The Road to Woodland

JONATHAN LOVEJOY

ISBN-10: 0692363262
ISBN-13: 978-0692363263

For every Caley

For this cause God gave them up unto vile affections: for even their women did change the natural use into that which is against nature.

Romans 1:26

The Other Side
of Dawn

My eyes are the color of the Caribbean Sea. My lips are the red of roses, as my makeup so desires, though the natural gold of my hair is unhindered by natural colouring. But what does it matter now, that my skin is as smooth as a porcelain doll's, as my former life fades into a background that is too dark to see?

The car's engine hums smoothly as I cruise along. It is no luxury piece—a stylish bit of nothing on four wheels, but it is new, and is the blue of oceans. As I watch the signpost up ahead, saying *You are now leaving Woodland Falls*, I do not curse my decision to leave my mother's infernal meddling. Nor the cloying, driving force of my father's weakness and judging eyes.

Past the sign lays miles of nighttime road ahead. The further I drive away from the edge of town, the darker this night seems to be. In the rear view mirror, the lights from the small city streets, the tiny Woodland skyline, begins to fade into the dark. Slowly.

Inevitably…

The lights fade.

Mrs. Ja'net Littledove had given her daughter an ultimatum. In her own words, she had reached deep into the Mother Line Reserves, retrieving "you will shape up young lady, or you will ship out." It had triggered the young woman in me, activating the calmly rebellious reply, *"Okay then. If that's how you want it, I'll call Aunt Wendy tonight."* These black, western Virginia skies bear witness to a night owl. Caley Littledove, and my decision to leave East Ridge Estates behind. I had not even accepted my father's guilt money, the Old Money, as he hugged me on the front lawn. "Call me when you get to the next town," he had said, which I most definitely was not going to do. I had planned to surf the night wave through every town between here and the Roanoke County Line, then onward to the Coast, to where plain, simple living Aunt Wendy would be waiting to take me in. Even now, I think warmly of her.

Maybe, I *should* have waited until the morning. The road is darker than I could have imagined. My twelve year old sister had mocked my stupidity for the night drive, seeming a little glad that I was finally going (or was it sadness?), or maybe, she just couldn't accept the fact that her sister's new car was loaded with one way baggage, and that I was really about to steal away in the night. Somewhere in the storm of her grief and confusion, she had seemed to understand—even while her eyes betrayed her sorrow, and a desperate desire to come with me. I glance out the window at the bright, brilliant stars above the houses passing by, imagining how much fun me and my brainy little sister would have had talking about them.

Is sixteen too young to leave home?

Are the rules of childhood and morality really as strict as they seem to be?

I brush a blonde strand to the side, and turn the radio onto country music comfort, the oasis of song and melody. I know this stretch of road well enough, from the many trips to the next town, because their Mall is the biggest and best this side of the Alleghenies. I say a fond farewell to the dead tree in the yard of the last poverty house, and make the right turn on Brewer Road. I am unmoved by the familiar patches of darkened trees and high grass. Rolling along in nervous leisure, enjoying the country station, even chewing my mind gum hungrily, knowing that my blue jeans could not allow a single meal between here and Virginia Beach.

Why did they let me go, if they think I'm too young?

They did it to hurt me—

Letting me risk life and limb on an interstate highway after dark. Knowing I would probably be driving in terror all night. Learning my lesson. Are they really waiting for me to call? Or have they had enough, because I had punched my little sister in the stomach hard enough to make her leave me alone for a week. Or because I had pushed my father, making him stumble back into my dresser, alarmed, amazed at how strong and angry I could be?

My nerves suddenly jitter at the sight of the last red and blue interstate sign. The big one. The one that lets me in on the truth, that independence is scary, and that decisions must be lived with and consequences must be taken. I travel onward, wondering why it has come to this, why I had to leave luxury behind for the journey east. This sixteen year old knows that she is alone now, as she approaches the onramp, curving around to the busy highway. The fear in my body tells me that I am too young to be this defiant, that it is time to get my stubborn shapeliness back under my mother's will, and beg to be forgiven. Maybe I should have listened to my mother, and taken a day trip. Or listened to my father and taken the plane. But then, I wouldn't have had my new blue Saturn to drive.

I wait at the onramp until there is no doubt, and then as the inexperienced young driver I am, slide smoothly, foolishly onto 64 East to Charlottesville, then the scant few hours straight to Norfolk by way of Richmond, then to Aunt Wendy's little house in the shore side town. Whether this is permanent, or just for the summer, nobody knows. Aunt Wendy is so nice, though. She understands me. She will let me be a woman. Let me do what I want.

3

I glide over the dark western Virginia Highways, headlights passing me unawares, as I leave Woodland Falls to itself. Undeterred by the black hills looming. Unmoved by the beauty of rhododendrons and sugar maples being left behind, caring nothing for cardinals, black bears and country roads of the beloved mountain state nearby. This surely has not been Heaven to me, almost nor otherwise. The rest of the world is waiting somewhere. Somewhere on the other side of dawn, beyond the mountains, and the Great Appalachian Forest.

With the radio blaring, and the comfort of other cars to guide me through, I pay the last toll on this part of the journey, confident in full grown beauty, loving the second looks and smiles from the toll men and women alike. I am free now, a fact made more apparent under the starry sky, as the sign welcomes me coldly into Virginia mountain country.

For many miles, the road stretches onward. Eons of distance, descending gradually, as the high ground begins to loom upward around me, on either side of the highway as I drive. Though I try to stop it, my mind replays every moment of the tension that had grown before I left. Rising, until it broke like a wave in the kitchen of our palatial house. It had gathered steam in my mother's body, driving her fuming from the big living room all the way into the kitchen to ask me "what did you say to me?" With my back turned to my longsuffering mother, I had answered calmly. Defiantly. Mrs. Littledove had glided across the kitchen floor, grabbing her daughter's arm, grabbing *my* arm and whirling me around, feeling (not seeing) a monstrous slap fall across her own face, which resulted in the only swollen eye she'd had in 37 years of living.

My rebellious, fiercely independent self listens to the voice of a country girl on the radio, drowning in static. If I am selfish, willful and stubborn, even a little conceited, is it really my fault? The world's response to me has been overwhelmingly positive from the beginning, teaching me that I am special, and that I deserve to be treated as such. If someone hinders my path, what else can I do but react? If I am not allowed to come and go as I please, what else can I do but run? Escape? I do suffer some guilt at least, when I think about my poor sister, and the pain I caused her with my bad behavior at home. If the family was in chaos, perhaps it *was* my fault. As for my father, I hardly thought about Mr. Absentee at all. I remember how glad I had been, even exhilarated, when I had pushed him noisily against my dresser that night. Thoughts of his plain, pallid face and tepid forcefulness makes my blue eyes squint, and my red lips tighten.

The country station suddenly begins to fade rapidly, until the song is buried in static. I switch the radio numbers up and down, letting it scan itself, finding nothing. Maybe, a little quiet is best right now anyway, because I begin to wonder whether or not I am still on the right road. The big, four lane bypass had vanished at the last restroom and soda exit, and I have followed the arrows carefully along deserted back streets, praying for the sign that will lead me off this woodsy road, and back to a big, cozy interstate highway.

Azure eyes of bluest sky
Lips the color of Crimson

"*T*his can't be right."

There are suddenly no streetlights, and the road is winding through a dense, thickly wooded area. I am about to turn around, when the headlights light up the red and blue sign for the interstate. I breathe a loud sigh, thanking God audibly. Soon, the road begins to wind less and less, and the trees are scarce, until there are hardly any at all.

The radio sounds as if it might return to clarity. A voice tries to speak some comfort from beyond the haze. After another half hour of checking the dial, the static wasteland, I turn it off, wondering how it is possible that I can't find a single clear station. I pop in a CD, and then another, and then another, and then another, amazed when all I can hear through the speakers is a loud clicking sound.

Dad...

He would have gone with me to the dealer tomorrow, warranties in hand. What good is a car if you can't play music while you drive?

Something inside begins to pull at me. Prompting me to stop the car in the middle of the dark, two lane highway to nowhere and turn around. I've never felt more like the child that I am, wanting my father's company, and my mother's sympathy.

In the distance, every star shines brightly, down to every horizon. Far ahead, the bottom of the starlit sky seems covered by a range of ghostly black hills, seeming to stretch from one side of the world to the other. I check the fuel gauge, glad for three quarters of a tank full, and a pristine new engine. After a while, the dark horizon shape looms closer, larger, until I'm able to see that it is the edge of a dense mountain forest. I have to slow down a little, ready for the sharp curves that might jump out at me from inside these Allegheny Woods. But the road seems determined to keep me on the straight path. The woods are so thick, it is like a mass of pure blackness on either side of the road. I check the sky, and see that the stars above the trees are as bright as ever.

Suddenly, the woods vanish into the night behind me, and I am astonished by the expanse of flat terrain all around me, as if I were on a desert road. My eyes adjust as I drive onward, and I think I can perceive movent. I feel my body freeze, when I realize that the dark road has led me away from my trip to the light of new life, into the middle of a wasteland. All around me, cloaked in darkness is nothing but *water*, like a nighttime ocean, lapping gently against the side of the highway. The road is raised above the waterline, and there is no railing on either side.

Carefully. Fearfully. Inevitably, I slow to a stop. I can hear the sound of a massive silence, broken by the noise of calm, cataclysmic potential, splashing in the darkness against the nighttime road. Cautiously, I turn the car once, then back up, inching, remembering the driving lessons long gone, barely able to see the edge of the road from the headlights. Back and forth across the road, gradually turning, creeping, until the car is turned around completely. Then deliberately, fervently I begin my trip back down the road away from the water, toward the dense forest. As I drive back between the blackened woods, I am careful to keep the tears blinked out of my eyes. And though I can no longer see the water, I can feel it , lurking somewhere on the other side of the trees.

I drive on through the forest for what seems like an hour longer than before, until one side of it vanishes suddenly. There, off to the right is the dark water, disturbed by a rising wind, splashing harder against the black road, threatening to crash a wave across. To my left is still the black woods. I grip the wheel tightly, repeating aloud under teary eyes and a terrified expression: *"What it this! What is this!..."*

The car swerves in my confusion, and I turn strong towards the woods, slamming on brakes. All I can do is gaze to the right, through the passenger window, knowing, hearing that off the road is a dark, watery end to it all, if I should allow carelessness to plague me again.

"God help me God help me please... God help me please..."

I gather my wits, knowing that the way back to the interstate is somewhere along this road. Or is it? I don't remember seeing any water before. What is it anyway, a mountain lake? Seeing that the fuel gauge has hardly moved at all, I put the stylish little car back in its driving gear and set off again on the road to Woodland, back down the dark road towards the light again.

Her cheeks are lovely as the Rose
Her nose is sculpted angel's flair
The fairest maiden to abound
In this valley of shadow and silhouette

After several hours of tearful, fearful miles, the dark water vanishes from sight, and the forest around me seems less ominous and foreboding, familiar even. When the red and blue sign to 64 flashes in the headlights, I laugh in epic relief, thanking Heaven, praising Him reverently. Before long, I am cruising the same interstate highway I had come from, glancing toward the tinge of pale orange in my rearview mirror, watching the stars begin to fade. The first car I have seen all night appears over the horizon, and I breathe deeply, instinctively reaching for the radio dial, deciding not to turn it on. I open my window partially, listening to the wind whistle, breathing in the fresh, morning air above western Virginia.

With the fuel gauge fast approaching empty, the bright blue car is welcomed by the signpost to Woodland Falls. I have never loved the sight of traffic lights before, thinking that the red and green bear the beauty of flowers. The town has never seemed so bright and new, and so many of the cars were more beautiful to me than I have ever noticed before. As I cruise the sleepy morning town toward East Ridge Estates, I wonder where on earth I had gotten lost, and how silly I had been, overacting to an unfamiliar lake road. I feel like such a child, which suddenly very comforting. Regardless, I know that my reunion is going to be the stuff of fantasy, hugging my family robustly as the Prodigal, returning from the Land of the Dead.

Power drifts from the tree lined suburban streets as I roll along, cruising the Wealthen Stream, the energy of life and living. My own neighborhood is admittedly unfamiliar in this new light of hope. They have me. No more battles to fight. I will endeavor to persevere. Loving my childhood that remains, striving to be what every parent wishes their daughter is, and what they hope she'll grow to be.

Parking crookedly in front of the house, I ignore the strange cars in the driveway, and the dense fog in my head, the dreamlike, the remains of a stressful night without sleep. I pick up my pace across the manicured lawn, hopping up the stairs to the big, white door (*why is it white?*), opening it and running inside, hardly recognizing the décor I had never bothered to appreciate before.

"Mom? Mom I'm home!"

As I start up the stairs, I see my grandmother come out of the kitchen and stop dead in her tracks, opening her mouth to make a sound. Then a sound like the beginning of a scream escapes my grandmother's lips, and the sound grows until she stands immobile, screaming at the top of her lungs. Grandmother looks so young in her fear. So strange. Her clothes are different as she screams.

Suddenly, a middle aged man I don't know comes from the upstairs hall and stops where he is, saying *omigod,* covering his mouth with his hand. Their fear drifts, flowing though the room among the screams, infusing me with a sudden terror, as I slowly understand these two people are my *mother* and *father,* staring at the sixteen year old daughter they had not seen since the night I left them, twenty years ago!

Jonathan Lovejoy

The Mother Line

River

\

6

*A*ngela Tao Ling was my sister's name when we adopted her. Another privileged, prestige adoption of a little China doll by an American soccer mom, which raised no eyebrows when it happened, except maybe those of the child's real Chinese mother Lai Tao Ling, a former Chinese immigrant long since flown back to China with her husband. A "white market" baby, for all intents and purposes, where money talks and bullshit walks, and undisclosed amounts of money change hands every day among the privileged. In this case, those privileged with brains, beauty or birthright, to go with the heavy weight of money bestowed. Lai Ling Tao basically sold her baby to the highest bidder and went back to China.

And this was Ja'net Littledove in the right place at the right time, who took little Li Tao Ling before she was dry. The beauty and bustiness of little Li Ling's mother was a pretend non-issue, appropriately subjugated by both my mother and father in the whirlwind of desire, repressed by the hypocrisy that rules—where every motivation is above board, every action is a product of perfect motivation, all covered in smiles and sinister snickering submerged in silliness, with Raymond Littledove pretending not to notice the sheer size of what he had never thought possible on a woman when she handed them the baby in the hospital, having trained himself—along with the rest of the Tiger Woods worshipping, Trump Tower wishing tomorrow men—to pretend in the daylight hours that they don't notice breast size and beauty, while they abandon their lollipop headed trophy wives for the black or barrio-hipped maid in secret.

And this same feeling that the men are allowed to own, runs an invisible and unspoken current beneath the surface of Woman, where latter day women have given themselves over to the spirit of pure lust, all but abandoning the natural use of their husbands like witches in a forest, who ride the Sybian in howling nakedness under the light of a silvery moon. In this same undercurrent that flows, my mother whisked up this little Asian baby from that *"stupid Asian bitch"* of a mother, whom she had wanted to strip naked and tit torture to tears for no good reason but to get off on listening to her cry in Cantonese.

But this, she held under lock and key as she cried in the joy of new motherhood, condescending her exalted self down as the angel of mercy, more than glad to accept the bitch's worship, on her way west toward a slow boat back to China. More than once over the years, as the little Asian doll would grow, Ja'net Littledove would put herself to sleep at night with her dream self on top of Lai Ling Tao, biting her breasts and listening to her scream to the God and Christ her *"heathen country has rejected outright,"* she has said.

Oh, I have wondered so often, who is it that Ja'net Littledove prays to in the gigantic mega church every single Sunday morning, a coliseum sized arena so big that there has to be a giant screen up for people to watch if they want to see the pastor's face as he smiles and promises his way through another sermon like a politician, or as his wife prances in six inch pumps and Penny princess casual. Oh, what buxom blonde beauty art thou, Woman of the Cloth! In the heart of her soul's memory, my little sister, who was gathered up with the rest of the world, and Rip Winkled twenty years down the timeline — in the heart of Angela Tao's soul memory, she is the little prestige project, the little China Doll in the blonde white woman's arms, her eyes closed to the Laodicean goings on around her, as her New World mother holds her like a little bundle of gold wrapped in silver linen and luxury.

I see Ja'net Littledove. Draped over her daughter's back like a Japanese Ju-on. Somewhere along the timeline, so soon after I was gone, this spirit flowed down the Mother Line River, flowing the Ja'net Littledove, the Ja'net Curlingale family tree that grows. Roots tapped so deep into family violence and discord, that Janet spent her young life swearing that her life would be anything but—spending her days draped in the cloth of smiles and goodwill toward Raymond, helping him achieve his lucky lawyer fortune, combining it with her multi-million dollar inheritance from the Curlingale name, people that seemed to be rich without cause, wealth passed down by Fate along the timeline. Janet Curlingale married Ray Littledove in the spirit of hopeful determination, a far pressed effort that the violence she suffered at the hands of her mother in secret would not prosper in her home. And by this determined, direct assault on her will, she was able to push the spirits at bay for a time, the way that the woman whose mother was a whore and an adulteress can push the lust for other men away for a time—the way that a woman whose mother was an alcoholic can push the wine glass away for a time, Ja'net was able to push away her mother's spirit for a time, until after my sixteenth birthday had come and gone. It seemed that one day, whatever it was that had simmered in this pot had finally spilled over, when my teenage rebellion sparked a journey from her in a rapid walk from her bedroom to mine, and the pretty 36 year old woman turned the corner into my bedroom like an angry wasp and practically ran over to me and pushed me in the back while I was at my closet looking for a blouse. This woman 20 years my senior—twice as worldly, twice as strong, was suddenly standing over me like a pissed off tiger, threatening me with something beyond bitterness and discord. The fear and shock I felt held my tongue in check, so that I could not say a blessed word, thankfully, not realizing what level of negativity there was pending.

The heights and depths of this, that and the other thing passed down, suppressed and pretended to be forgotten—by hiding, lurking beneath the surface of who we are, waiting to be activated by the right word, the right look, the right gesture at the wrong time. The spit and venom in my sixteen year old mouth had come out on its own that day "...*well you can just fuck off then...*" I had said in triumph, sick to death of her rules and regulations, of her curfews and Curlingale control, telling me what I can and cannot do, where I can and cannot go, who I can and cannot see. For the second year in a row, I was asked to be a cheerleader, this time by the varsity squad, where for me, Caley Littledove, for goodness sake—for me, tryouts would have been a formality. Jumping and dancing and smiling with half the enthusiasm of so many others, but surely that was not going to matter. It was not a glorified dance team. It was an old fashioned cheerleading squad, where our job was to hop and bounce and smile, wave our pompoms in the cold, frosty air of November, to warm the cold hearts of wayward matrimony in the lustful souls of women and men.

I wanted to be a cheerleader. Mother said no.

"I will not have you jumping and bouncing around half naked for a bunch of football players. I said no and I mean no and that's final."

And this was where the Curlingale spirit entered our dimension, the door that opened, by where it was able to pass through this portal uncovered. Something so benign, so insignificant as whether or not Janet Curlingale's daughter could become a cheerleader—this was the place where the spirit had rested in grieving for sixteen years after I was born, waiting for time to move us along to where it waited patiently. And this portal into our hearts, into our minds was opened when I spoke the fateful words. Activating the evil, sadistic temper passed down the Motherline River. I can remember the thickness in the air around us, the immobility in my arms and legs, the soul of vitriolic hatred glowing in her eyes, the inner knowledge washing over me that told me not to move, that would not allow me to move, lest the unthinkable occur. Even now, I can picture that alternate happening in that bedroom, that might have had both her hands buried in my blonde hair, where I might be wrestled to the floor and punched in the face until the room began to haze around me.

This, I know could have happened, as it has in so many homes around the world, where mothers have allowed the curse from their generations to uncurl like an angry sky in a storm. And I wonder, why was I spared the impending onslaught of the Curlingale mind, this spirit passed from mothers down to every generation of her bloodline—why was I spared the infinity of fights, beatings, whippings, canings, and every manner of secret punishment imaginable? Why was I lifted from the flow of this reality, to a place undreamt of by the Einsteinian mind, where this three hour tour was not the stuff of silliness and island comic fantasy, but a dark and twisted reality unearthed to me, where perhaps so many that have suddenly turned up missing have come and gone? I wonder why I was pulled into the abyss of this other dimension, why I was pulled into the waking nightmare, which allowed me to escape 20 years of something that surely would have built up to a bloody tragedy, and the burning of fire and brimstone in a mother and daughter's life.

How was it that I was spared this dark reality, that was moved over to my twelve year old sister when I left, which began almost to the day the sun rose over my ghostly departure. The very next day I was gone, I am aware that mother dropped the pretense, and the China Doll she once loved to play with suddenly became a *"disrespectful little Asian bitch,"* when Ja'net suddenly had no tolerance for her little Asian daughter's pretty little smart mouth and attitude. It began the day her relationship with me ended, when Aunt Wendy reported that had never arrived, commencing with my little sister's: *"Its your fault that she left. You were always punishing her and yelling at her for no reason. You're mean and I hate you!"*

Oh, what innocent anger! What naïve negativity is that of the twelve year old China Doll, who knows not from whence the whirlwind cometh! In the heart of my sister's memory, she can remember the sound of her bedroom door opening and closing so quietly that day, and mother walking so calmly over to the bed where her daughter was sprawled in twelve year old weeping repose, turning her over and sitting on top of her, this grown white woman, sitting on top of her pretty little Asian daughter, who was too pretty and smartmouthed for her own good—turning her over onto her back and laying heavy down on top of her, twisting her ear hard enough to make the little Asian girl scream, then with her other hand, covering her mouth completely.

There, she lays on top of her daughter. Understanding only that the feeling that courses through her body must be obeyed, and that every muffled squeal, every kick, every pulling at her by her daughter's weak little hands builds one energy wave onto another, until she feels as though she might be lifted from the bed, and carried through the walls of her suburban estate into oblivion.

Caley Van Winkle was what Angela said in awe and grieving, after my father called her to drive back to Woodland. He had smartly refused to tell her on the phone, but made it clear that it was imperative that he come home, telling her on the phone *"I need you to come home now, honey."* I can remember that Dad was the calm in the storm of my arrival. The sanity in the midst of chaos. Because what my mother was seeing—the sixteen year old sight before her eyes—was something she refused to process, something her mind simply could not, would not accept, as it always is with what is known as the Third Part of the Truth, which is Cataclysm. The loss of control, the loss of autonomy, the loss of ownership over what happens in our lives is the most devastating bomb to the rich. It is the kryptonite of the privileged. To learn once and for all that you know nothing. That you came from nothing. That you are nothing. And that you're always going to be nothing.

The arrival of the inexplicable, the unchained element unleashed is the undoing of the rich and powerful, who secretly cower at the flash of every bolt of lightning, and tremble at every blast of rolling thunder in the clouds. The reappearance of a daughter she had given up for dead, 20 years to the day she vanished, and having not aged a single *hour* in the process—it is something that her mind will not allow. As if to acknowledge it is to acknowledge that there are forces beyond her control. To acknowledge the existence of Fate, Destiny and God. Fear of Poverty, Fear of Public Shame and Humiliation, Fear of Pain, Fear of Failure, these are among the types of fear that haunt the rich and the powerful. The beauty of man's creation, the twinkling lights of the cityscape at night, the towering skyscrapers that glisten in the light of day—these are the manmade glories of the privileged, the appreciation of art and talent, the glorification of beauty produced by the hearts and minds of men. These are the corridors of cultured civility, the halls of the haughty and the hallowed places. A world crafted by men, to serve men. From boardrooms to bedrooms, and every deep and shallow place in between, these are the spaces that we control, the places we patrol in dominance and subjugation, in power, privilege and performance preplanned and executed.

These are the hallowed halls of logic and reason. The exalted palaces of human rationality. What is hardly known, what is rarely discussed or believed, is that the wealthy are often terrified by the unexplainable, horrified by the unobtainable. Discomforted by the inspiration of nature. Unsettled by the power of the sunset. Put ill at ease by the rising of the Moon. Unnerved by the twinkling field of stars across the dark'ned sky at night. Scientists have conquered this fear, with calculations, explanations and the like, so they don't have to fear the shadow of the Moon, when it passes between the earth and the sun. Oh, but what explanation can there be, when the sixteen year old girl vanishes away, and returns 20 years to the day, having aged nary an hour along the way!

In the heart of memory where I live, I see an extremely beautiful, hourglass shape of buxom Asian beauty walk in, who can only open her lovely mouth without words, and cover it with her lovely hands, when she looks at the girl who was once her *older* sister, that left this house in sorrow twenty years before. *Caley Van Winkle*, are the words that come out on their own, when the sister who was twelve hugs me in power and beauty, in weeping from Asian eyes of thirty two.

9

She is the most beautiful woman I have ever seen. Whether this is bias on my account, I chose not to know. As this Asian flower drifts us away from the house of pain, east of the road to Woodland, I can barely focus on the evening road in front of us. I wonder if anyone has ever tried as hard as I am at this moment to see out of their peripheral vision, as I make a warlike effort against my instinct, which has my head trapped by the invisible, to try and move it to the left, to make me stare into the profile of this deeply Asian beauty. The woman who drives us in silver Sonata semi luxury is a woman, to be sure, with two of the largest, darkest eyes, that hypnotize as they blink. Her pale skin is as smooth as porcelain, to contrast the length of shiny, silken black hair that falls long past her shoulders, to a portion of the top length of her back. The scent of her is sweet as the honeysuckle, to delight the breaths I take every so often, to remind me that scattered throughout the field of corruption, there rests an occasional Armageddon flower in bloom.

Angela Littledove. Angela Tao Ling. Professor Angela Tao, PhD in Astronomy, gifted with the profound memory for text and trivia, to disguise the average cognitive intellect in the above average memory processor. Having skipped the tenth grade in the years when I was gone, due to pure test taking prowess, content in her typical disappointment of the scientific world, who praised her as the second coming of intellect itself, but cushioning her fall from the heights of academic and scientific expectation. *I'm not really that smart*, she always told them, *I just have a good memory.* But oh, Lady Tao, how can they leave you be! How can they not anoint you as the arrival of a new Queen of Letters, a Goddess of Learning, when your eyes, your smile, your name, the sheer size of the bosom you carry, the hips echoed from the Kardashian Land, how can they not anoint you as queen of their wildest hopes and dreams! The world's most beautiful book worm, Miss American Nerd Girl, I see. Your awkwardness, your natural shyness, so deeply disguised in outer beauty that is truly disturbing to be near. How many hopeless longings have you crushed over the years, my dear sister? How many hearts have you left shattered to crystalline powder, and scattered to the four corners of the earth and wind?

"I'll say it just one more time," she says. "Then, I promise I won't anymore."

I used this as an excuse to turn my head to her and stare.

"Caley Van Winkle."

She has to remind herself that she is driving. So as not to stare over at me for too long.

"If I was worth anything," she says, "I'd have already made phone calls. Prepared myself for an end-of-the-world feeding frenzy."

"You mean me being dragged around the country on a freak tour."

"At least. But something inside me won't let me do it. At least, not now."

"If not now, when? You would have to do it while I still looked like this. Prove to the world that I am who you all say that I am. I couldn't imagine what might happen if people found out."

"Truth is, honey, I think that maybe, at least for a while, you would become the most famous girl in the world."

I look away from my sister's aura, to gauge that of the fading light, as the earth turns toward the evening day.

"Its almost over."

"What's that, honey?"

Almost unable to answer, I take a quiet breath, ready to exhale whatever answer there is for my tragic soul to give.

"Time."

Jonathan Lovejoy

Autumn of the White Woods

10

Swirl precious harmonies in righteous pearl

Where the Spirit of the Lord doth rule the world

Comet sensibilities will give this a whirl

As the eve of the Second Coming of Christ unfurls

11

What is it that your colleagues through the years, Lady Angela, what is it that your colleagues cannot know about thee? What did your teachers in the eleventh grade choose not to see, my dear Angela Doll? All they wanted to see was the beginning of what they called a "stellar academic career in the making." They pretended it did not matter to them, that the awkward Asian girl was bent over in the loose T shirts and button down collar shirts under the weight of the heaviest breasts in the entire school, though you were but a girl of sixteen—the heaviest breasts the school had ever borne witness to—even greater than the church bosom of the hefty black teacher with the big body besides. Though your body is normal size, the bosom you carry is macromastic, a topless photographer's most impossible dream, and this, upon the body of one so young and unknowingly blessed with prettiness about the face. They don't know what to make of you, do they, Ms. Littledove? Though you are the school strange duck, that *pretty Asian nerd with the big tits*, they all say behind your back—though you are the school geek, you smile your fungalooga smile of social cushioned comfort, having walked the rose petal path of positive experience from your peers—even from your smart little spelling bee winning days of elementary and Jr. High school, through the ninth grade when you rarely missed a question on every test you ever took, to when Ms. Bullock, our church bosomed Betty herself, recommended you for testing.

The tenth grade was no longer an option for you, was it Angela? But oh, my dear sister, what is it about thee, that the teachers and the other students don't know? What end of the world truth is it about thee, is it that they refuse to know? It is what the scriptures have warned of ad nauseam, that the world refuses to accept or believe, that will remain taboo and unspeakable, even while the walls of secret are being torn down, so that the world may see the truth. The ultimate truth, the last and greatest part of the truth that mankind is evil. The last and greatest part of the truth that woman is wayward. This is the autumn of the white woods, Angela dear. The death of innocence in your home at 16, four years after your sister vanished from the world we know. What is it that the world will never know of thee? Ja'net Littledove, sister dear, is the tragic secret I see. Who still haunts your waking memory, nearby the age of thirty three.

What do they know of thee, Angela, my sister? Of what you have been cursed to deal with in the summer of your sixteenth year, just before the beginning of your early eleventh grade season? Of the girl burdened with brains and bosom, cursed to believe that her body is warped and misshapen, they did not see when Ja'net waited until Raymond Littledove was on his next two day trip out of town that summer. They did not see, nor could they imagine, that your smiling, *White And So Pretty* rich mother was the source of what is reserved for the pornographic mind, so pervasive in fantasy, and even moreso in our hidden realities. They did not witness you and she at the mirror of her bedroom, in front of the rare and beautiful golden oakwood mirror, of a beauty and uniqueness hardly witnessed anymore across the length and breadth of the furniture industry, where Vaughan Bassett was given the keys of this upper class eschatology.

Your teachers and fellow students do not see what I hear and see, Angela dear, of Ja'net Curlingale's quiet and determined removal of your bra, far upwards of the key of G Major, where some mother's have ridiculed their daughters into the reduction surgeon's butcher room. No, they are not witness to the path chosen for you by Fate, when the woman's blood boils in end-of-the-world perversion, to where her mouth is parted slightly open in awe unrestrained, unashamed as she makes you stand in your white underwear with your hands behind your back, that she may marvel at the echo of what she remembers from your birth mother, and of what she had never believed or thought possible before. *A million dollar chest*, is what she says, as she takes up the old fashioned wooden ruler she blesses God in her heart that she was so lucky to find, making you stand still and upright, with your hands clasped so tightly behind your back, that she may study the nature of macromastia, then the nature of sadism unrestrained.

Your teachers do not know, do they Angela dear, that she put the ruler repeatedly to thy bosom, that she put the ruler to your nipple in one quick whack after the other, until you had to open your mouth and let the cry flow out on its own. They did not hear Ja'net tell you to *stand still*, and to *keep your hands behind your back,* while she focused on the one nipple, until she had broken you down to a scream too loud for her to allow. They did not see her place the ruler on the dresser, while she took her dress off, and then her bra to expose her own D cups dangling, They did not see her get behind you and put her hand over your mouth, and commence to play a melody born from the generations upon the front of your breasts, a rhythm in rapid 4/4 time, carried along by the muffled screams from within. They did not see your mother, dear Angela, when she was no longer able to play the Pitty Pat Chorus in tit for tat, when she gripped you from behind in a hug about your waist, leaving your gigantic breasts exposed above her arms. They did not hear your mother's voice, dear Angela, when the moan slid out of her throat like the low, hopless wail of a mountain ghost, a phantom of the woods. They did not see your mother, dear Angela, as her body began to shake like a jack hammer, to tremble such a beautiful quiver into that low, quivering moan of hopeless agony you hear.

No, Angela. They did not feel her breasts mashed against their backs. They did not see her breasts mashed against your back. They did not see the long and dreadful quiver of the motherline hips spread to infinity. They did not see her hand at your throat, dear Angela, nor did they see the weeping anguish upon her expression, nor did they see the tears flow down both your faces in the tragedy of slow, steady streams.

*I*solation greets us with open arms, upon our arrival at her country estate. A smaller version of the two story brick palace she grew up in, to be sure, but landscaped by green, open space—with a long, black asphalt driving path from the road to the house. As we make the green grass turn, rolling the lane to her country prosperity, I have to remind myself that I am in the presence of the girl I once punched in the stomach because she wouldn't leave me alone. As the row of cedar pines rolls so uncasually by our window, I am blown away again by the fact that what I remember about us is from yesterday in my spirit, while in hers it is a memory born from 20 years ago.

Under the clouds that have gathered in grieving, we disembark our rolling chariot, me with not a single bag or suitcase, having left everything—the car, the clothes, *everything* back at our mother's house. Angela had made a hasty retreat for us, telling our father that we would be back later to get my things—all of it still stored and tucked away in the abandoned shrine that is my bedroom, kept up all these years by my grieving, nostalgic father, who had protected the memory of me from becoming part of the dusty corner of the attic. I suppose the sight and smell of me was enough, everything about me being time warped in her vision, like the image of a childhood relative pulled so vividly out of a dream.

As I stand at the front of the two story brick refuge, taking in the infinity of this country lawn, the grass cut to golf course green, I can feel my sister's effort, my *older* sister's effort—her refusal to give in to the spirits of fear and confusion, having the strength of character to accept the impossibility of me with integrity. She strolls over to where I am, hiding the pain of bewilderment that seeks to burden her beautiful features, putting her arm around me in genuine support, as if to answer a calling from somewhere beyond this madness, to protect this little freak of nature from the reality of the nightmare she is in. *Rescued,* is the feeling that dominates me from top to bottom, like a flood victim pulled from a raging river, as we turn away from the open space of the prairie green to go inside.

My sister's home is a monument to intelligent décor, unburdened by feminine foolishness nor masculine mischief, but is a sea of books and darkwood shelves, offset by the time precision of every kind and character of clock known to man, with the occasional tree or palm plant grown in its artificial authenticity, with plush, cushioned chairs and sofa of the loveliest melancholy gray. If a library or a museum could be made comfortable enough to live in and call home, this spacious living room is it, drawing my attention to the 70 inch monster of a television screen, surrounded by books and shelves of all kinds of quirky intelligentsia, dominated by the presence of beauty in wood and string.

"Do you actually play this?" I say, unable to resist touching the shiny violoncello wood.

"I'm Asian," she says. "What do you think?"

My sister picks up the heavy wood and light bow string, both of which seem so much like benign house decoration, and less like the voice of an angry God to an endtime generation. I watch this beautiful Asian woman settle into the nearby chair, handling the lady instrument with such skill, leaning it back to herself in the glory of its calling. The beautiful Asian places the long bow to the string, moving it across the violoncello wood, and I suddenly hear the voice of eschatology, moaning its somber voice of beauty, as sung from the mind of Johan Sebastian Bach those few centuries ago.

In the lady cellist's movement of her fingers up and down the top of the stringed place, as she moves the bow so smoothly across the lower region of melody, I hear the sorrow of the ages for an endtime generation, from the Cello Suite No. 1, the Prelude so appropriate in the key of G Major, to honor the bosom of the sixteen year old girl she once was, who was called to this diversion when I was away. I watch the fire maiden express this sorrow from the prelude, listening to the tension build toward the ripe conclusion, where in lies the third part of the truth arisen from the tree of Eve, which is Cataclysm. And then, I watch the woman whose beauty rises from the East, burning blue and black fire, pull the bow across the face of the cello one last time, where the end of the world is whispered on the G string.

When I blink, the haze of mist I didn't know had gathered is suddenly cleared, tickling as a single tear down my cheek that I quickly wipe away, unable to speak a word to the fire maiden, of the message I just heard in royal blue and alabaster evening song.

13

The song of the cello sings this melancholy tune. To carry me up and backwards along this twisted timeline, to the twisted motivations, across the forests and fields I know, to where I see the sixteen year old girl I never knew. The young Asian beauty with the macromastic bosom, suddenly dedicated to the rise and fall of scales as they are sung by the cello wood and string. This, after she learned that we are at the end of the age, and this is the eve of the Second Coming of Christ, as it is foretold by human behavior. Behind close door depravities that I have been called to see, sights and sounds I have been chosen to hear, to absorb and reflect by the tragedy of recollection, as I am moved back and forth along the River of Time, nearby the solemn edge of this precipice, nearby the end of human history.

By what I am cursed to know, I can see my beautiful sister on the morning after, having dreamt of the cello's voice in her unblessed sleep, after she endured the fire in her breasts, the sting of our mother's ruler at her bosom. Cursed to have joined the unfortunate hoarde, the unknown and unnumbered many and few who are hidden, who have come to finally understand that to be born is to be cursed, and to live is to suffer.

I see Angela Littledove. I see Angela Tao in her morning shower before school, sixteen years old in the fall of her eleventh grade year, a year younger than most of the other students, but tragically, so many years less naïve and unknowing. I can feel the startling, the dreadful spark of fear that shoots through her in the bathroom when the shower water is turned on, and the space around her rings suddenly with a knock on the bathroom door.

It's me, comes the voice of Ja'net Littledove, mouth so close to the closed, locked borders of her desperation. I see the young Asian beauty hurry into her towel, going over to the door in rushed effort to not know, in quick motion of forced non-understanding, to open the door in pretend innocence, staring at the lovely blonde, upper 30's, upper middle class suburban queen who is her mother.

Mother stands still for just a moment, refusing to allow ignorance into her own expression, cursing pretense away with a stare, into the loveliest Asian eyes she ever knew. Hiding the smirk and smile, in the calm of quiet, fevered understanding, Mother places her hand on the door and pushes it slowly open, refusing to take her eyes from those of her daughter.

In the morning of this slow motion haze. In the reality of this dream come to life, Mother so quietly closes the bathroom door behind her, in the early hour before her daughter goes to school, amidst the voice of the waterfall behind the crystal shower door, and the steady arrival of early morning steam all around them. The look upon this woman's face calms to a determined acceptance of her fate, sliding her robe off her shoulders and letting it fall to the floor, then removing her daughter's towel, to witness the rarity in nature, a famous photograph untaken, of the Asian girl of sixteen, and the most disproportionately large breasts that can exist in natural shape and beauty.

"That's impossible," she says aloud, unable to look away from the sight of them, taking her daughter by the wrist somewhat firmly with one hand, placing the other at the small of her back in full control, escorting her over to the raging waters of this morning shower not yet taken. Mother climbs in this oversized tub, oversized hips exposed, pulling her daughter in after her, oversized tits burning the blood of the Curlingale heart and mind.

I see the lovely woman near 40, with soap and lathered suds in her hand, rubbing it in circular motion over the breasts of her daughter, swallowing the mouth watering instinct unbeknownst, unable to fathom how a body can exhibit such profound pleasures from within. I see the beautiful Asian girl before her morning school routine, staring at the blonde woman with hardly a blink through the fear, terrified of what twisting, what biting, what pinching agony there is to be had in this shower, and the silent charge to keep silent, so that none could hear, so that none could know what level of pleasure or pain there must be.

But Fate would have mercy upon her skin, as her mother, as *Mother* rubs and squeezes with such depth of feeling and understanding, that it conjures a spirit of relaxation, and a raising of the daughter's hand to her mother's breasts, to where her nipples have arisen to what peak of attention they know. The mother and the daughter are at war with these sensibilities, with these that flow through them and between them, that raise the mother's plateau to rapid unendurability, and she must suffer the humiliation of a quick lightning strike, which causes her entire body to twitch beyond her control, wobbling her one single, mighty spasm, to turn her face red from the failed effort to resist what has happened, as she must begin to take deep breaths in recovery.

In the haze of this slow motion dream. In the heat and steam of my sister's memory. I am privy to her soul's recollection, and the death of innocence at the end of this age, as I watch her rub our mother's breasts in full, massaging them as Mother holds on to her daughter's gigantic bosoms without a further motion, feeling her Asian daughter's hands massage her breasts with patience and natural skill uncovered, watching the ivory return to her mother's lovely skin in full, blissful recovery.

Song of the Cello

Jonathan Lovejoy

*T*hunder rolls over my nighttime recovery, in the bedroom prepared for my country arrival. I am still stunned. Unable to emerge from the drowning waters of my memory, of what it was I have apparently fallen prey to. As the new storm declares its endtime purpose over our country estate, I am barely able to accept that I am awake and in real world space, and not the ghostly product of some dream I cannot escape from. With my sister's help, through the song of the cello, through what wonderful dinner there was prepared and eaten, through the long, luxurious bath and nighttime repose, I am at least able to hold onto my sanity, as I slowly begin to process the fact that yes, I am real, and no, this is not some silly suburban nightmare, where I will awaken from safe in my tenth grade bed of youth and uncaring.

From what I gather, from my features, from my memories, from what I am told, I am definitely still sixteen, haunted by the ghosts of yesterday, which roam the world I remember from 20 years back along the timeline. To be sure, Fate will have mercy on me and wake me up from this delusion, and Ja'net Littledove will call me down to breakfast in bitterness that I will not return this time, or ever again. Surely my little twelve year Asian sister will be at the table with me in her exotic, impossible little eastern beauty, biting her breakfast in the morning happiness and hunger. Surely, my father will rush through the kitchen in one of his suits, to get to his glass of orange juice before going to the office, where he will sit all day at his desk and work at nothing for one half of a million dollars per annum, the only name a law firm called Littledove and Associates needs on the business cards to draw the clients in. Surely, this world I remember is but a sunrise and a brief awakening away, to rescue me from a destiny altered like no other.

But in this nighttime rumbling from the clouds, I am reminded again that for the accursed, there oftentimes can be no salvation, and no deliverance from suffering. Of this truth, I am suddenly compelled to accept, glad for my luxurious surroundings, and the comfort of the woman who I know to be my sister, the little twelve year old girl I once knew. I am again burdened by the power, by the tragedy of what she has come to know behind the walls of secret, of those things which cannot be imagined, that she can never speak of to another living soul but me.

My dear Angela is the accursed sixteen year old, after her awakening to the Curlingale blood, the depravity passed down through my mother's spirit to her. It is the Ja'net Littledove blood that burns, the curse of this perversion passed down, so that even I have felt its calling myself, though not in full understanding, but able to understand my mother's past obsession with my sister, the depth and intensity of which has lasted even to the present day.

Oh, my dear Angela, what is the pain of this modern mother daughter dynamic that torments thee! Of what has the fifty six year old woman and your thirty two year old self been such a prisoner to! Of all of this, of all these things, Angela, thou canst hide from me no longer, as I am called to know and understand every part and particle of thee.

And of this curse bestowed to thee, I can see its full flowering begin when you are sixteen still, after you awaken from your night dream of the song of the cello, letting you know by what means you will hide from the world, by what public mask you will hide your face of tragedy in. I am witness to Angela Tao's embracing of the cello when she is sixteen, when you are sixteen, Dear Angela. You submerse yourself in every verse and nuance, every sound and séance of spirits conjured by this instrument, as though you will somehow, someday dazzle the world as heir to Jacqueline Du Pré, to flow the latter day winds of the Harnoy mystique, to give the cello means by which to carry its somber message to the world.

I see you in the shadows of false hope, my beautiful Angela, having mastered the instrument by sheer force of will through your junior year, in such full support from mother, who sees this public façade for you and she to hide behind as such a godsend too good to be true. And typical of the rich, public minded sensibility, Ja'net goes at this at 100 miles an hour, as if you will become the Eve to Yo Yo Ma's Adam on this instrument. In your senior year, when you turn seventeen, Mother locates for you a private teacher of the instrument, for students with the promise of talent over money, whom you have to audition for before she will take you on.

This woman is tall, strong in her extreme and sensual Armenian beauty, colored by a Greek-Italian heritage, having played in orchestras under two of the world's greatest conductors, retired after thirty years of thunder and lightning on the instrument, content and complacent to spend the rest of her beautiful life as the dutiful show wife, and beautiful mother of two daughters. This Amazonian beauty queen, whom we must call Adelia, to keep her anonymity as the barrier between her and the eyes that stare. I see you at the so-called audition for this strong and exquisitely beautiful woman, whose features are so deeply reminiscent of what would be Jewish, Greek or Italian.

This dark eyed woman, whose soul is arisen from the heart of creativity, whose mind burns the fires of artistic expression, this lady cellist watches you, Dear Angela, having seen the haunted forest of her dreams call to her in reality, as the living ghost of her blood sits astraddle the instrument she was born and bred to play herself, watching this Asian goddess have the audacity to play a solo andante from Rossini's Duet for Cello and Double Bass, and have the greater audacity to inhabit space in front of her as the living embodiment of her deepest, most desperately hidden and unspoken dread and desire.

As you sing the Italian aria for cello, too slowly and without its plucked bass-line accompaniment, she can hardly hear a word the instrument is saying in the audition room around her, as she stares at her living China Doll's hair, her eyes, and the unbelievable size of what bosom she is hardly prepared to believe in. Of what so-called audition is this, for the rich woman's talented seventeen year old Asian daughter, whose technique is but merely promising at best? What so-called audition is this, where the sound of the cello has faded to insignificance, to her most profound ambivalence, as she can surely not take a breath from the sight of watching you play?

The tools of artistic expression are displayed in power and beauty. Either this, or they are displayed in vain. For what is the purpose of a so-called audition to the jaded Adelia mind and body, if it is another spoiled little prodigy hardly big enough to hold the cello steady, stroking the strings in such robotic perfection beyond their years? Of this expression of melody she sees, is the power and beauty of Woman, in the young body of this Asian girl, who draws her stare so completely past the cello itself, to the face and body that sits so naively in place behind it. Adelia listens, she looks, having already cursed in her mind the many long seconds she has left to wait before the Asian beauty is finished, and she can tell her how glad she will be to take her on as her prize student and possession.

Sometimes, truth is stranger than fiction, my Dear.

How dare you cross my path! You rich little Asian cunt!

In the Armenian woman's eyes, dear Angela, I can see the resentment grow to its Diluvian dimension. I can feel the swirling of emotions in her, my dear sister, swept down on winds of inevitability, gathered upon winds of lust, and the release of a lifetime of longing unseen. Here you are, to dare inhabit space in front of her as the embodiment of her life's secret desperation exposed, the nightmare of her own lust unrequited, the Vesuvian eruption 30 years in the making. Unable to sit any longer in front of you, dear Angela.

I see the beautiful Armenian, forty some odd years in worldly maturity and sensuality, stand up so smoothly in her deepest midnight dress cloth, walking over to you as you finish the whirly Italian notes of the restless Andante you play, of the strange duet you have transcribed to solo for this audition. What does it matter to the lady cellist, this jaded world traveler, this voyager to every musical world above and beyond the call of duty, having played music fit for kings and queens, of princes and princesses, of caliphs and royal concubines—of what importance is your amateur technique to she! This woman burns in an end-of-the-world flame, that has arisen up from her repose, an encouragement in your mind that she is greatly interested.

This heavy breasted, heavy hipped Amazon, this modern queen of the arts, steps so unlively, with such quiet purpose over to thee, dear sister, circling around behind you in the spacious audition room, where the sound of your cello is a brief echo from the walls of secret. You perk yourself up in the sitting stance, as your fingers work the top of the giant strings, as Rossini's madness continues to mock the both of you, until at last, the swirling bow goes silent, and your fingers take over upon the lower strings, and you pluck the pizzicato in one single stretch of 4/4 time. These are the notes descended as the single word of warning, dear Angela, one word spoken four times, North, South, East, West.

From the one note plucked four times from this whirly-winded Andante, you do not hear the warning that is spoken. You only feel the unfathomable at your chest, in deep squeezing from behind you reached around, while both your hands are occupied at the big instrument, as though they are bound invisible before thee.

You cannot drop the big bow string to the ground, dear Angela. You cannot let the cello fall noisily to the floor. So you hold on for what life there is left in thee, as the strong, feminine hands—the squeezing—long enough for you to look so fearfully to the side, where all you see beside you are the focused eyes of Armenian beauty as they stare down over your shoulder with purpose, as you feel the squeezing force move to the buttons of your burgundy dress cloth, undoing them in determined, rapid succession.

Oh, but what is the nature of fear, dear Angela! Making you have to call foolishly her name, *"Miss Adelia?"* A connection established early on upon your arrival at her palatial home. Miss Adelia Evanopoulos. Touch thy hands to glory! This truth, my dearest Angela, is so much stranger than the fiction they know! Of this, the world will not believe, my dear sister, to dismiss it as a fable of fantasy!

Of this fantastic truth, dear Angela, I see at your dress cloth in determined skill—the strong, beautiful white hands sliding down past your bra cloth, holding on to the bra with one hand, while pulling the great breast out with the other, until your right breast is completely spilled out and exposed.

You have to whimper *"Miss Adelia"* just one more time, don't you? This, to bring naught but irritation to the Evanopoulos mind, to add fuel to the fires of her will. The squeeze of her hand, of both hands to your gigantic breast is of a feeling unknown, a violation unimagined, even so far beyond that of the Curlingale blood, whose perversions done in secret have not prepared you for this reality.

Already, my dear sister, you are an accursed woman. A dog to be abused and kicked by life. A despised untouchable, to be used and spat upon by those who deem themselves superior to thee. You are nothing, Angela. But a China flesh doll to be groped. Used for pleasure. To be an outlet for someone else's pain.

You hold still in this impossibility. Lovely Asian features twisted with shock and melancholy, as both the beautiful hands now hold the gigantic breast of yours up, as the beautiful older woman leans forward over your shoulder from behind and clamps her mouth upon your nipple. As to the feeling you endure, as to the wave of energy that courses through your soul, you do not know. It is drawn from you in the deep sucking, the uncompromising pull of your nipple into her mouth. As to the feeling it raises in your groin, you do not know. You only know that the kneading of this woman's fingers, the feel of her deep sucking at your breast, the sight of her mature beauty in this perversion, every slow bobbing of her head raises an ire in your body that threatens, until it *strikes,* causing your entire body a single, mighty twitch, a spasm born from somewhere you do not know. It is amidst the sound of a great clatter to the floor, as the bow finally slips from your hand unbeknownst, which spurs her onward to a deeper commitment, as you seek to recover from the unwanted violence to your soul, mind and body.

In the knowledge of your body's devastation that are the spoils of her victory, as she takes the rest of your dignity from the single, great breast exposed, grunting one, two times without shame in her deep voice, Estros strengthened by the feel of Testros, and the power of the whirlwind channeled through hardline femininity.

She releases the divine breast in one final, kissing pull away. Turning her deep kiss to your mouth, still leaning over you from behind, in full control of what tragic future you have left to give. To double up upon you what truths and tragedies you have already been made aware of, and will continue for a brief lifetime of sorrows.

The taste of her tongue is sweet as sugar, and as lemon yellow as the burning sun.

Upon the sweetness of this kiss, in the aftermath of trauma, your instinct is arisen beyond pretense, and you deliver to her the prowess of a tongue kiss, shocking in its commitment, and glorious in the manner of its depraved depth and beauty.

A vitriolic rise and fall of sound cascades as the voice of doom, rolling rapidly along the rain soaked nighttime Virginia countryside. Any hope I may have had of sleeping in comfort has suddenly passed into oblivion, causing me to feel as though the waking nightmare I was in has somehow swam up from the waters of a dark yesterday and night, to swallow me into an unbreatheable space of fear. Sanity is at once a fleeting memory for me, abandoning me for a brief moment or two, until I have to sit up and try both to breathe and remember where I am.

In a haze of brief recollection, I slide onto the carpeted floor in something like quiet, desperate awe, in rapt amazement of my inability to remember who and where I am. A blast of this nighttime thunder flashes my sister's beauty into my spirit just enough, allowing me to follow her ghostly memory through the lonely country house, down the upstairs hall to her bedroom.

I open the bedroom door without the late night pretense of a knock, noticing that my hand on the knob displays a visible tremble. *My God, I'm shaking,* is the thought that forms and dissipates on its own as I creep into my sister's bedroom, walking through the dark over to the dark wood canopy bed, the four corners rising to their towering height of corporate luxury. I imagine that my sister's hair is shiny in the dark, whether I can see this silken glow or not, her head turned opposite from where I'm standing, her head barely exposed from under the plush, royal burgundy cloth comforter. Color barely comes forth in the dark room, while I am unable to unfreeze my fumbling, fearful stare and hopeless longing. But another bright flash of warning and war from these night clouds shocks me into action, and I lean over and quickly touch her on her shoulder sleeping.

"Angela," I whisper, shaking her with enough determination to bring her back to the land of the living immediately. Because the prospect of going back into that room alone is the same as if Regan's Demon from *The Exorcist* is waiting for me in the closet.

My heart is fluttered with hope when she turns over to try and see what creature hath conjured her awake, her face unpuffy with sleep, and still extraordinarily beautiful in the dark. With such a prowess of understanding, with such a commitment to what is real, without a word, she turns the covers back and beckons in the storm, for me to climb down from the heights of shock and fear. I crawl into bed beside her, instinctively facing away from her, feeling the soft, curvy length of her body pressed full against the back of me, with her arm wrapped tightly around my waist.

With memories of that nighttime forest and mysterious, eternal sea still enveloping me from the inside out, I take comfort in my sister's arms like a weary traveler, invited into a warm shelter from the icy, winter cold. She speaks nothing of my cold skin, shallow breathing, nor the trembling I am suddenly unable to hide. She only grips me tightly around my body in the dark, raising up, leaning over me to press soft, warm lips to my ear in a quiet moan, that seems to flush warmth to my entire body, then takes my earlobe gently into her moan of mercy, pressing another moan in kissing to my cheek that makes my trembling cease to be.

As I drift away, in the arms of this end of the world compassion unbridled, I am again swept into the heart of her soul's memory, where I see the great breasted cello teacher on her knees on the bed, opposite her great breasted Asian cello student, both on their knees in the bowels of secret, locked into the deepest kiss imaginable, face to face, the cello teacher's Olympian breasts exposed and hanging down over her black blouse cloth pulled down, her tight gray skirt slid and bunched up at her waist, black stockings tightly in place, the lace tops of them halfway up her thighs. Her hand holds the back of her Asian student's head in desperation, to lock them together in this impossibly deep kiss, where their tongues are hidden in their endless search for pleasures unknown. Both the teacher and the student have their hands at each other's underwear, rubbing feverishly, as if racing to the top of this peak to climb, breathing desperately through their noses for life—the Asian girl's other hand not behind her teacher's head, but clamped at the teacher's nipple in a motionless, mighty pull downward, per the teacher's specific and desperate plea and instruction, to *just pull it down really hard but don't mov*e, that the pleasure might be delayed in its ultimate arrival. The two of them, on their knees facing each other, locked in this forbidden kiss and passion, this unfathomable dynamic unseen and unimagined—the two of them are locked motionless from head to toe, save for their arms in a feverish and unbreakable rhythm, where the hands are at the center of each other in desperation, until the Asian girl adjusts the pinch and pull on the woman's nipple the tiniest bit, which changes the woman's breathing dramatically, causing her to double over from the lightning strike at her breast and groin, and the explosion of power at the center of her body. The deep kiss is hopelessly unlocked, as she must bend forward, grunting deeply in bursts of animal sounds just short of bellowing, as her Asian girl student continues to rub her depraved desire without mercy.

Jonathan Lovejoy

Eyes of the

Bear Lion

This storm grows its uncompromising intensity, stretching the miles west of our country farmland East of Woodland. In the palatial, Virginia estate inside Woodland Falls, Ja'net Littledove is a prisoner in the mother daughter brackets of her timeline, vacillating in the cycle of fear and rage, both emotions gathered up and spread out forward and backward, from the woman she remembers from childhood and deep into her adult years, where what they know lasted in secret until her mother died at the young age of fifty six, a heart problem grown to its full, dark flowering in the night. The beating, the behind closed doors raping started when Ja'net turned sixteen, the age of demonic consent, when all bets of innocence are off for every demon on the timeline. In this family tree, the fruit ripens and falls upon the sixteenth turn of the seasons, where the motherline fruit falls at the foot of the unrighteous tree.

Ja'net Curlingale Littledove lies underneath the storm. Dreading the onset of her mind's involuntary recollection, and what passing through the years it must entail. Ja'net remembers the fire of Jane. The Curlingale fever that was wrought. Jane Curlingale. Mother of three. Ja'net, Jennifer and June. Three beauties raised under the cane and the lash, in the shadows of Pentecost. Fanaticism born up from the country farmhouse in the mountains of this very state we live and die in.

Jane Curlingale. Newly rich. Loyal to husband and children by show. Steeped in bitterness by spirit. Jane Pilgreen. Jane Curlingale. First Assembly show wife. Mother of June, Jennifer and Ja'net Curlingale. Sworn to marital chastity bound and tied. Purveyor of unspoken witchcraft about the palatial house and home. The witchiness of marital dominance through sexual denial and threats of bitterness unendurable. Wife of a lowly medicine company millionaire. A million saved over ten years, ten million more from lucky stocks gone wild. Mrs. John Curlingale. Jane Curlingale. Mother of three.

Ja'net Littledove flinches at the voice of doom. Ticking of the clock of fear. A pricking of it in her soul tonight. Fear of what has been done to her from somewhere in the wilderness of her past. Terror of what ghostly sixteen year old that reappeared. In fear and grieving, in rage, in bereaving for what must soon be passed down. From Jane. To her.

To me.

The word whispers an echo through time. A word that my mother remembers. A word that Ja'net remembers.

It is a word spoken in the wrath of man. The wrath of Woman. A word simultaneously embraced and rejected, both loved and feared. This is the word that Ja'net remembers speaking to her mother, after the seasons had passed her sixteenth year. A word born of its own accord. Almost whispered. It is the magic word. The key to this portal in time, through which the spirits of what must be may pass.

As Ja'net Littledove listens to the storm, every flash of lightning is a flash of memory. Of every blow her mother delivered to her face in slapping. In the maturity of their dynamic. Screams that were kept hidden from the father. Hidden from the sisters who are away. Screams delivered in a house devoid of life, of listening ears, of what curious hearts and minds would pry. Ja'net remembers her own hands tied behind her back, her body stripped to her underwear bottoms, her skin and breasts laid bare. Ja'net remembers the fire in her mother's eyes, the fire in her brain, the fire burning her face to ruin. The pain of swollen eyes and cheeks, the sting of a lip split open to blood.

As the thunder rolls, Ja'net remembers the weight of her mother laid down on top of her, the heat and stale moisture of her mother's breath in her face. The pain of her mother's teeth at both her nipples, until she could not breathe from the pain. Ja'net remembers the aching in her wrists, when the stocking ties were cut. She remembers staring at the edge of her mother's bed, her arms crossed at her waist in weeping. Ja'net remembers that the types of fear are many, and uniquely distinguished. Among these is the Fear of Rape.

She remembers the look of stern control. Of absolute and somber look of depraved melancholy, of heightened sorrow and sanity in her mother's expression, as she straps on the long, thick member without fear. Without the shadow of remorse on her features. Ja'net remembers the nature of fear born in the brain, and the icy spread of it throughout the body. Ja'net remembers the sound of her own voice in pleading. The glimpse in the mirror, of the white of her own eye marbled to blood. Ja'net remembers the uncompromising, farm girl strength flowed through her mother, the

Amazonian strength blossomed. She remembers the tragicomic *turn your ass to me, bitch*. Spoken by the Christian woman. In the shadows of Blue Ridge Pentecost.

Ja'net remembers the deciding threat. The threat to be tied up, whipped, caned and paddled to bruises and blood. In the calm of uneasy acceptance, in the pain of victory forever lost, in the thistles that grow east of Eden, Ja'net must turn her widened hips to her mother. To endure the call of seventeen strokes of the paddling wood. Seventeen strokes, she promises. No cane. No belt. No ropes, twine or socking nylons to bind.

Turn your hips to her, dear Mother. Turn your hips to our mother in grieving.

Ja'net remembers the rise and fall. The sifting of agony through the forest leaves, the whistle and whisper of messages in burning. Ja'net remembers the pain of the paddling wood, and the burning of blue and black fire. Skin raised to a bloody welt at merely seven strokes. A welt to cut her white skin to blood. Screams and a call to God for deliverance. To incite only harder, more determined strokes to seventeen. Then, the truth of a lie unfolded, to stream pleasure through the wires of the sadistic mind. To hear the daughter's pleading, the begging, the crying upon another seven loud, agonizing swats of the paddling wood.

Ja'net remembers the twenty four. The twenty four steps to oblivion. The twenty four fiery steps to Pompeii. The burning of fire and brimstone upon her skin.

Ja'net remembers the recline. The repose upon her stomach on the bed. The anchoring of her hands between her own legs. The touch of the rubber plastic at her rectum. The tension. The tightening of her entire body in futility.

Ja'net remembers the first scream. The scream of death. The death of innocence. When the thickness of depravity was passed into her body from behind. She remembers the splitting of a barrier. The breaking of what seal was forbidden. Bowels on fire of midnight and blue. A scream born of its own accord, as the member is pushed to its completion.

Ja'net remembers the weight of her mother's body. The feel of her breasts mashed against her back. The pressure of the pain up into her stomach from behind. Pain made worse by the squeezing down. The raising up. The squeezing down. The raising up. This down, up motion on top of her from behind. A motion that refuses mercy. A motion made rapid in its tension. Through the haze of tears and agony. Through the maze of pain and fear.

Ja'net hears breathing above her. Breathing that suddenly has a voice. A voice that calls to *God and Holy Jesus* for mercy. A voice that wails in sorrow for the ages.

Ja'net remembers the quaking. The shaking infinity, laid on top of her. The aching in her bowels.

A mother's voice in weeping.

The center of perversion swirls the Angela Tao mind and body, the vortex of this vice passed down. Having been burdened two fold, by the sicknesses of two different women along the way, so that she is unable to maintain this platonic pretense of my protection. Even in the safety and comfort I am blessed with from her, safe inside from this otherworldly storm and wind of eschatology, the heaviness of what burns inside her is as the gravity of an approaching object from space, which has an effect on her spirit unwanted, drawing her into the motion of what must forever be. The inevitability of this motion causes her to squeeze tighter against me as the thunder rolls outside, until the curtain of her own hypocrisy must fall.

In the revelation of secrets unfurled, I am shocked to awareness by the electricity of discovery, sparked by the pinch of her fingers at my nipples, followed by the deep pressing of her groin against me from behind. But I am overcome not with fear or revulsion, nor some self righteous pretense of puritanical resistance. The nervousness I hear in her breathing, the hesitance I feel in her touch, the reticence in her body's squeezing overwhelms me with something akin to compassion, as I know that this is a part of her bestowed unwilling, and is a part of her that cannot be stopped.

As these end of the world winds continue to blow, amidst the flashes of lightning and blasts of thunder, I am privileged to the arrival of a spirit from somewhere along the timeline, having chosen my sister as its conduit, whereby it must pass itself through her to me.

I am sixteen, when the spirit comes to me. I am sixteen, when this end of the world spirit hath come.

I'm not the least bit afraid, when I finally turn over and stare at her in the dark, but able to see clearly the worry in her expression, that rises to the level of pure apprehension. "I'm sorry," she says, in genuine regret and defeat, which I deflect with the assurance that no, I don't want to play those coy games either, and yes, I understand the fire that burns.

It is the taste of wine from one person to the other, where one feels the twinge of life, fluttering their heart and every nerve ending from head to toe, at the foot of a family tree of wine gluttons, drunks and lushes to infinity—where the other feels her body's resistance and revulsion to the taste, with their nose wrinkled in disgust, and every taste bud in shock at how something can be so unpalatable.

But the touch of her finger to my nipple, married to the pressing of her breasts against the back of me doth ring the chimes in me from head to toe, and though this beautiful Asian woman is my sister, I lean forward in the dark to the full lips, to finish in my body what she has started, and to deflect her worry somewhere into the nighttime storm. This woman twice my age, I can feel resisting a visible tremble, as she allows herself to cross a line she had never known she would approach, as she allows herself to embrace the forbidden. It is my first kiss, where I am spared the ugliness of masculinity in my face, or the bitterness of maternal depravity unleashed. The feel of my sister's lips against mine does something to my body that I am truly unprepared for, causing me to take a deep breath through my nose as I lean forward against her, lost in the cushion feel of her kiss in the dark.

In her, is the arousal of guilt and fear, merged with my exhilaration and naivite, that sparks an explosion of feeling between us, that transforms her resistance into something forceful, where she has to usher me onto my back. The next flash of lightning truly does show me her new expression, which is no longer the pain of apprehension, but frustration, and the need to release a sudden pressure in her mind and body.

I understand that I am suddenly captive, physically dominated in quiet by the beautiful Asian woman, who undoes the buttons atop her silken night pajamas in pure instinct, and pulls the two gargantuan breasts out for me to see, in the nighttime storm of our desire. In the rains of this awakening, I am held prisoner by this nighttime vision, as she pulls my T shirt up just enough, to expose the perky, firm B cupped itty bits of mine. With her giant breasts still exposed, I watch her lean down to pull my nipple into her mouth in a quick, deep sucking, causing my whole body to twitch from the trauma, and the words *oh my God*, to come out from me on their own.

In the haze of this slow motion dream, in the maze of this slow motion reality, my mind is lifted upon the winds of violence that blow, to carry me upward and downward, forward and back again, until I feel as though I might fly through the universe at the speed of light, to be carried from Earth to the shores of Heaven.

As if she can feel this devastation threaten, as if to ward off the scream building up in my body, she releases my breast in mercy, in a hard, kissing pull, moving over to the other in this selfsame magic of a nursing, suckling pull. The same, quiet cry to *God* escapes my lips, as this pleasure too is in danger of a transformation, causing her to pull away again in ingenuity, to save my body's energy built up for what needs there are she may require.

The beautiful Asian turns over on her back, ushering me on top of her, refusing to speak as she stares at me, while I clumsily move past the great globules, the gargantuan globes of flesh, up to her pretty mouth again, to rest my clumsiness and dimness to her mouth in lust and grieving. Before long, she can endure no more, and gently pushes my head toward the Great Bosom, where I am as one who is thrown into the deep end of a swimming pool for a lesson.

While laying on top of her, I take the two breasts into my hands, lowering my lips to one nipple without knowledge, unprepared for the feel of her nipple sucked deep into my mouth, and the apocalyptic shock suddenly born in my body. The sight of her naïve, blonde little sister out of time, clamped at her breasts like a starving child, expression burdened by a pleasure deep enough to cause pain—the sight of this rings truth from her brain, to her bosom, bowels and empty womb, through her legs and feet, to somewhere in our space nearby.

I am as a woman dying of hunger and thirst, whose face is buried in the sweetness of a watermelon, where the swallowing is both to eat and drink at the same time. At the place where our groins meet, there is a motion I must begin, even while I am buried in her bosom, sucking each nipple in turn, while squeezing, mashing and wobbling two of the biggest, fattest breasts in God's creation

The pathetic bump and grind of virgin hips commences on top of her, my silken night shorts firmly in place, with my T shirt rolled up to where my B-cup sponges hang so ready and exposed. Not knowing why, with no understanding of what instinct shores I fly, I am compelled by the unseen to straddle her, but hardly able to let the breast fall from my mouth. But when she touches my nipples with both hands, my mouth opens, to cause her big breast to wobble free, making me sit up to position the straddle, working my hips in a quick and powerful slip slide, stopping long enough to lower my head like a woman wooden bird at water cup, grabbing her breast into my mouth and pulling it up so mountainous and high, letting it fall noisily from the sucking, wobbling back to its rounded place below. The great globes are so big and rounded when she is flat on her back, wobbled so impossibly in roundness that seems to go on forever.

I suddenly am unable to stop looking at them, hump sliding myself against her as I stare, almost afraid to move too much longer, afraid that I will not be able to contain the scream building up in my body. The fever flows from my heart and lungs, to send knowledge to my lips in motion at her nipples, causing me to pull them up to mountainous heights repeatedly, letting them fall back into place. I can tell by the look of anguish, the desperate frustration on her face that this is an untapped vein, a mother lode of perversity for the Asian breast queen, to have someone sit atop her in service to her, in total submission to her, with one of her gigantic breasts pulled up in sucking to Olympian height by the nipple, then released in the loud, sucking, popping sound.

As I pull the great breast up into my mouth this time, I find that I am unable to let it go, and I am unable to stop my hips from doing The Virgin Slide, the slip slide of the girly grind, gripping my whole body in motion until I understand that flight over this cliff cannot be stopped, as the scream in my body is muffled by her gigantic breast sucked into my mouth, followed by the sound of an Asian woman's scream in full, deep siren and sorrow.

"This is an end of the world storm. You can feel the electricity in the air."

In the morning aftermath of trauma, I am at rest at the breakfast table of my future, 20 years fast forwarded from yesterday, living and breathing the ghostly waters of Einstein's most iridescent dream. I have been sixteen forever and a day, still coming to terms with what has happened, whether or not I am actually awake in this endtime reality. The beautiful Asian woman, the sister I have come to know, stands unashamed in her black sports bra and matching stretch pants, clothes that surely would be underwear if she were in public. I watch the unearthly Professor Tao gaze out the massive, country bay window at the mist and gray, her mind as much on fire as is the top and bottom of these clouds that glow.

"I've never seen a storm like this," she says. "Its like being at the heart of a hurricane, yet its just a thunderstorm. A local one at that. But its getting bigger, they say. Half of Virginia might be under this thing by tomorrow. And they say there's no end to it in the foreseeable future."

I stand up from my sweet and sinister sausage and waffle sin, angry at how even though the orange juice had been sweet and perfect, I insisted on eating the waffles with syrup anyway. I curse this sweet and sour compulsion, standing up with the glass in hand, walking over to the window where she stands in secret, shapely Amazonian curves and beauty.

"Aren't you gonna eat?"

"My tits are big enough as it is. One meal and I have to starve for days."

In the wake of Mischief's compulsion, my free hand is suddenly raised, palm extended, bringing it down definitively across the rounded, wide ride of a backside she hides.

"Sorry," I say, humiliated by the slightly shocked, judgmental stare. But in keeping with who she is, with the woman I have come to know, she climbs down off it, pressing those soft lips to mine, with a determined moan besides, vibrating me in a line from my lips straight down.

"I'm the one who's sorry, honey."

"Why?"

Angela Tao stands up straight and true. Un-plain. Un-ordinary in Amazonian stature.

"Some sister, huh?" she says, gazing again past the stormy window, both of us drawn to the violent gusts of rain and wind.

"What do you mean?"

"Even after what you've been through, this end of the world impossibility. Even after the nightmare place you've been, and the one you're still so obviously inside of, I treat you like something out of Camille Cosby's worst nightmare."

"What?"

I suppose the bewilderment on my face is epic.

"Honey, you're a Child of Destiny. You're a sign of the times. You're darn near sacred. And all I cared about was how I felt. I didn't stop to think for one minute what something like that would do to you."

"What? Because I fucked my sister?"

She stares at me again, but this time, hiding the burden of revelation behind the most enigmatic, poker faced expression in the world.

"You heard me," I say. "And I *meant* it. And I meant it last night, too."

In that beautiful, so uniquely Asian manner, she looks down and away, watching me the periphery, while turning back to the rain soaked window pain. Though she stares out the window into the storm, I can still feel her gaze burning right through me.

"There's a flash of the girl I remember," she says. "You always were older than your years, weren't you?"

"That's why I had to leave home. Remember?"

"I remember you punched me in the stomach so hard I thought I was gonna die."

A twinge of impossible regret twists my insides, as if reached from a great distance, and wrought by ghostly hands of judgment. I am compelled to suddenly put the bitch in the Curlingale blood away forever, stepping away from the bitter hands of discord that threaten in this storm.

"Please forgive me," I say, stepping up against her, my orange juice arm around the small of her back, my other hand tight around her waist. "Please forgive me for leaving, and for treating you so bad when you were little. I swear to God I wish I had never done those things. I was just mad at Mom and I took it out on you."

She finally breaks the periphery, and turns to stare at me in the compassion I have come to know.

"I love you," I say.

The tragedy of who we are stands us together at the window, in the shadow of dragon fire from the clouds, and bear lions made of rain, with glowing white eyes that stare at us in the storm. As if conjured by the kiss and hug of two deviants in the country, two of these white eyes emerge from the driving rain, driving down the long, black asphalt driveway.

Unable to say a word, unable to voice the depth of fear, the two of us can only cast one long, last stare, a last grasp of fleeting hope, as the black luxury SUV rolls in full, hearse-like glory near the front of the house.

The Asian Amazon takes the orange juice from my hand, gathering a renewed strength I can see and feel, as she walks across the big living room, past the cello in repose to the dining table. My attention is divided by this tension, as the beauty in extreme walks back from the table in quiet battle mode, in time to join me, to see the appearance of a figure dressed in black, emerging from Hell's Chariot, walking un-rapidly through the rain in her long, black coat and matching umbrella, as if enjoying a gentle, rainy stroll in the park.

Angela and me are unaware of the rising tide of tensions, the kind that take the breath as the arrival of a cold splash of water to the face, reacquainting us with the notion that the types of fear are many, and uniquely distinguished. Among these is the fear of humiliation, which accompanies the presence of so many who walk the world in strength, allowing them to prey on those who walk this self same world in weakness. We stand still, in the life giving throes of one last deep breath, listening to the door be touched and fiddled with so briefly, then unlocked with such smooth and abject skill and purpose.

The voice of eschatology screams a million messages undeciphered from the heavy rainfall outside, all gathered under the gray canopy of the same end of the world truth and cataclysm. With no word, and hardly a glance in our direction, we see the middle-aged woman of stature remove the black rain cloak and hang it in the closet, and place the long umbrella upright beside the closed closet door.

The blonde woman is a queen. A suburban W.A.S.P. of latter day, new world beauty, bound in the whitest button down blouse tucked in, inside a gray skirt stretched across hips spread to infinity. This woman's beautiful, mature face grows more stern, more somber as she walks toward us, until she stands up straight and tall, her own substantial bosom towering above the Olympian breasts of her Asian daughter.

"I don't remember giving you permission to take her."

The fearful display on Angela's face is a miracle of non-verbal communication.

Satisfied that her 32 year old daughter remembers her place under the hidden sun, Ja'net Littledove, Mother, turns a self-assured, pleased expression toward me, head tilted in mocking, staring me up and down in oppressive, overwhelming disapproval.

"I suppose it wouldn't do any good to ask you where the Hell you've been? And why the Hell you look the way you do. What, did you get abducted by aliens?"

"Mom, please…"

Only a look.

Only a stare…

Burning in blue and black fire.

Only this gaze, from the blonde woman to her oldest daughter.

This gaze.

This stare.

"Take off your pants," Mother says. Staring me directly in the eye.

"What?" Angela asks. Hopelessly.

"How do I know its really Caley? And not some twin somebody's trying to hoax onto me in some crooked scheme?"

"Mom, how can you ask that? Don't you remember how you reacted the second you saw her?"

"I said, take off your pants."

There is nothing that I can do, beyond obedience. Not remembering exactly why she would ask this, I undo my jeans in frustrated defeat, sliding them quickly down—

"That's far enough," she says, stopping their journey to the floor, just above the knee, to where the whole part of my snow white thighs are shown. Mother kneels down, such a powerful figure of feminine strength in her skirt, blouse and heels. She opens my thighs like a prison matron from Cell Block W, where end of the world woman is wayward.

The scratch of her nails threaten to dig deeper into my inner thigh, mercifully stopping for a moment, a brief moment stretched out to infinity. Mother stands up again, slowly, like a phantom ghost arisen from the deep, to claim those unfortunate enough to be nearby and among the living. The look on her face is the third part of the truth. Which is cataclysm.

"What *are* you?"she says. Burdened with fear. Fear that rises a barrier of angry protection within.

Mother grabs me by the sides of the head, squeezing my face, yelling questions I cannot decipher, until my sister steps so bravely in, prying herself between us, able to hold our mother's strong hands at bay.

"I won't let you have her," she says. "Don't waste your time with it 'cause its not gonna happen."

Mother calms herself, staring bewilderedly at her Asian daughter, allowing a spark of awe to color her expression. Mother takes a deep, strong breath, turning toward the window, strolling over to where the picture of endtime sorrow is framed by our country, upper middle class luxury.

"I don't know how in God's name this happened," Mother says. "But I know it's you."

"How?" Angela says.

"The scar," she says, without looking away from the storm. When you were twelve years old, I caught you choking Angela, remember?"

Strange, what the mind chooses to remember and forget. If she had asked me this before yesterday, before the Road to Woodland, maybe it is something I wouldn't recall. But since I returned, my heart, mind and body are ablaze with memory—burning the theater of my mind, consuming my every waking hour, until sometimes I feel immersed in a dream, flowing from one reality to another.

"I made you strip to your underwear," Mother says, "And I gave you the whipping of your life. And later, I saw you fiddling around with your inner thigh. And you showed me that bloody scar. It healed to that half moon shape that's still there…

"Caley."

Mother turns around, arms folded over the tight blouse bosom, walking slowly, strangely to where we stand.

Waiting.

"Pack your bags," she says. "You're coming with me."

With not a single word. With only a slow, determined shaking of her head *no*, my sister steps in between my mother and me.

"You must be out of your fucking mind," says Mother. "That little bitch is a minor, and she's coming home with me."

"Is she a minor?"

"I don't know how, but you can see that she is."

"Yeah? Well, I think her birth certificate and driver's license say different."

"You always were a smartmouth little—"

As if whispered to, as if reminded by a voice within, Mother's face is overcome by a sudden calm, a sudden, deadly reassurance. A self assurance that no matter what it takes, no matter how long, whatever mountain of resistance this is will be dealt with, and heretofore, the tunnel through this great rock will be carved just as well.

"Angela, can I see you in the kitchen?"

"We can talk here, Mother."

"Angela...can I see you in the kitchen?"

Without asking again, the woman flows away on a current of quiet, simmering rage unseen. Angela assures me not to worry, that I'm not going anywhere, and that she'll be back in a minute or so. The hot Asian woman follows the hot, older blonde woman, both figures gliding through our space in shapes so powerfully, and so distinctly feminine.

I would like to follow them. To listen to what fearful threats and promises, what tearful regrets and resistance there may be. But aside from my mother's deep mumbling, and Angela's voice raised at the words..."so you can do the *same thing...*" I wander away from them, back toward the window of endtime despair.

Before long, I can hear the older woman losing control, letting the calm slip from her voice, until I hear something about "this house" and "bank account... then *turn around*!"

A deathly quiet descends. Followed by a deep, woman's scream of pure pain, but this, not the pain of ecstasy unbridled, but of agony.

The second wave of this terror forms the words "it h*urts*!" into the air, sending a chill up my spine. This three part sonata of suffering ends with a final scream, punctuated by a pathetic sob of defeat.

After another moment of deafening silence, one enveloped by an infinity of rainfall outside our window, I see the beautiful, hippy older woman appear from around the corner, heels clip clopping down the hall, then silently across the big livingroom carpet, then clip clopping again onto the entrance hall by the door.

I wait breathlessly for her to look at me, to motion at me, to speak words of tragedy to me, concerning my departure from Paradise. But with hardly a glance in my direction, the lovely blonde lady slides into her raincloak unbuttoned, then gathers up her umbrella for a quick, angry trip through the front door and out into the rain

Framed by the massive bay window, I see the picture of wrath and power, stepping un-lively through the storm. Upon its departure, it is still a figure dressed in black, gliding through the angry storm as a worthy extension of it, climbing into the black SUV, where the lights of it soon appear as eyes of the bear lions made of water, turning away from the house, replaced by the eyes of bright crimson red, that flash brighter as they move away.

When the SUV is gone, I move slowly toward the kitchen, unnerved by each step as if trapped in a dream, waiting fearfully for the arrival of whatever waits around the corner in the kitchen. But I am pulled along by loyalty and concern, both powered by morbid curiosity.

I take the steps around the corner into the kitchen, where my heart is suddenly aflutter, shocked by the presence of the strong, deeply pretty Asian woman sitting in a chair, her arms crossed over her Great Bosom, while her face is twisted and wet with tears of a quiet weeping.

Rape of the Amazons

21

*I*t is the tragedy that so many wealthy sons and daughters suffer. The pain of subjugation, of emotional oppression—the misery of being trapped by the human need for money and security—holding them prisoner to the emotional whims of their rich parents. Men and woman touched by God in some special way, blessed with either beauty, money or charisma, or some combination of the three, who have their children lassoed in the ropes of this pride—this inexhaustible well of earthly satisfaction, where a fountain of prosperity feeds their children's lust of the flesh, lust of the eyes, and lust for the pride of life.

"We'll have to try and keep you a secret for a while," she says, the side of her face leaned against me, while I stand directly in front of her.

"Because of Mom?"

"She said she would cut me off like a dead tree. I'd lose this beautiful house. All the extra money she gives me."

"So what? You're a college professor with a degree from Yale and the University of Virginia. You don't need her."

"My school doesn't have a million dollar trust fund hanging over my head. She does."

"A million dollars?"

"When Grandpa Curlingagle died, he was richer than everybody realized. He left Mom 10 million dollars. Almost everything. All of her sisters think he left it to charity. They got nothing compared to her. If Grandma had been alive, Mom probably wouldn't have see one penny."

Understanding falls in deep revelation. From the storm clouds high above, through the mist of pouring rain. Down in spirit through the roof of million dollar country luxury, to where I stand in front of a trained submissive, in emotional and financial shackles for life. *In the hands of a sadistic beast,* is the thought that burdens the heart and mind, as I am tormented by what goes on behind the walls of secret, and the life of Angela Tao, the days of Angela Littledove.

My mind is lifted on these un-gentle breezes. Drifting through time, until I am drawn to the wealthy home in East Ridge Estates, where the walls are so often filled with her fervent screams. More unimaginable than this end of the world journey I've taken, are the screams that fly from the mouth of torture, from the face of beauty twisted to pain and terror. This, on the far edge of her latest experiment, where her 21 year old daughter is home from college, on a lonely trip undertaken by duress, the stress and pull of money and privilege, and promises of love ungiven.

This latest experiment of Janet Littledove's has her Asian daughter in the nude, held underneath her strong mother in screams and screaming, notes played upon the biting crest of desire unleashed, by the woman who must bite down on her daughter's breasts hard enough to draw tiny spots of blood. I can see the beautiful Asian woman, the junior in college at Yale University, having all but abandoned the cello as a hope for the future, still captive in her other secret as the teacher's lover in private—I see this prisoner of depravity on her back, held so tightly by the older blonde woman, a woman of about forty five at this time, biting the breasts of her twenty one year old daughter.

Of whom among us hath been equipped to believe, to suspend this barrier of doubt raised up, to accept that among the privileged, when the lights and cameras are turned off, lust and carnality are turned on, in secret displays of the lascivious mind in bloom, where the Lord himself hath said in scripture that it is a shame for us to dwell upon. But of these shameful secrets, I am cursed to know, as I listen to my sister's violent screams, and watch the disbelief in her eyes wide open, as she lies pinned underneath the rich, blonde woman, who has now taken to sucking the nipples hard enough to make the girl feel like she has been stung by wasps, then biting them to continue this pain to blood. This, the tiniest taste of it at Janet Littledove's lips and tongue, to satisfy her into moving to another place to drill upon the mountain, to find another pocket of silver agony to feel. Her daughter's tears, her daughter's writhing, doth raise the Curlingale Ire, this curse of woman passed down, to where the girl cock she wields is an inch times four in arousal.

Yes, this is the far edge of breast torture, to bring the woman to the front edge of Amazonian rape, the possibility and gift bestowed to so few women, whose lady member grows to a power unseen by man. This arousal is as a drug to them, an addiction they must feed, praying to the God of their loins for a victim, for someone to come along that they can feed upon, who can give them their fix of screams and agony. Whether or not this spirit is born or bred is immaterial, only that it exists is relevant, that through the deviant it feeds, it lives to draw suffering from the mind and body of another. It is the natural unrighteousness of man and woman concentrated, focused and brought to life, to explore the nature of pleasure enhanced by pain. This is the pain of her daughter's screams, which are not laced with begging for mercy, only that she be granted the strength by God and Christ to endure.

The energy of her daughter's screaming vibrates the Curlingale blood, to wreak havoc upon every nerve ending, to make her entire body an instrument of doom, a weapon of destruction and depraved, desperate domination and desire. When her daughter's screams have done their thing, when they have done their ding-a-ling tingly, the mother enters her girl cock into her daughter, in the Amazonian Rape, the rape of the Amazons, where the four inch clitoris is allowed to rest still, so the mother can look down at the weeping face of the daughter who is hers to control, to dominate, to subjugate both mind and body. The pressing of her daughter's great bloated, bloody breasts underneath her, the glimpse of the bloody bite mark at the top of them mashed up to infinity, the last glimpse of her daughter's beauty before her eyes have to close on their own, these are sent to her own nipples and girl cock grown, until she understands now that the spirit which lives in her has been fed to satisfaction, and will now release the reward into every inch of her body. The daughter rests thankful in the mother's tight grip, glad to at last be witness to the war cry of the Witch's Crown, that weeping orgasm that invades the body without motion, to rise the victim to a place above consciousness, where they cannot even perceive the scream they hear as belonging to them. This woman begins the high pitch siren wail, that betrays her mind's disbelief and shock, that such a wave of pleasure is possible for the human body to endure. The beautiful daughter lays underneath the screaming woman, the wailing woman, listening to the sorrow of the ages, perceiving the waves of pleasure, tormenting the mother's body in slow, steady streams.

*B*ut the violin teacher is gentle, is she not? Hers is the soft, secret contrast for you, Dear Angela. A breast fetishist extraordinaire, she is. Having kept it bound up these many years, keeping them tightly mashed and bound against her body under her dresses and blouses, so careful not to arouse attention to them—content that they must add weight to her frame as she disguised them in navy and black, keeping them hidden behind the cello, keeping her beauty hidden behind the buns of legend; hair pinned up in a ball, or swept up and stylishly pinned.

Adelia has always been pretty enough to be comfortable in her busty skin, not afraid to wear her glasses in public when it suits her, carrying herself in such tall nerdiness, such non-sensual, deceptively frumpy manner—where the long skirts effectively hide what lies beneath, as do the loose blouses and dresses, where the macromastian things are allowed to lay as flat against her body as she can make them under the tight, humongous bras. Bras that she dares not don to lift them or push them out, lest she give away her secret, that her frumpiness has nothing to do with her waist, but is because of what hangs bulbous down to her waist unseen.

With this woman, dear Angela, yours is a relationship so profound, that it will stretch seven years across time, from seventeen to twenty four, when your graduate studies matured you beyond her grip, and further into the sadomasochistic grip of our Mother. But while it lasts, is the seven year itch of the breast queens, a uniquely sensual exchange along the secret history of successful, suburban women, where she trained the two of you together to build up, hold, and release every drop of sexual energy through foreplay, and the kissing and sucking of them is the Milkmaid's Intercourse. And this powerful, protracted love affair is the stuff of private legend, the beautiful, exotic Armenian frump when clothed, in pairing with the shy, Asian girl of like extraordinary manner and appearance, both of who hold their prettiness in a determined public nerdism, the cello teacher and the academic, the lady cellist and her Asian student, having discovered one another behind the walls of secret.

Oh, what these unprivileged eyes hath not seen! What these unprivileged ears have not heard, when the cello duets you play are silent, and the voice of female to female breast sex is played instead! Oh, how they are not privy to the sight of these depravities, where you learn the truth of breast sensitivity, and how some women are cursed with this blessing. Who among us can imagine your phallus strapped on, where it is between her two great breasts mashed together, where you tirelessly, endlessy push it back and forth, in and out through the crevice of her bosom, while she sits on the bed in front of you, or lies on her back, you pressing them together with your hands. I can see her having worked herself to satisfaction as she sits in front of you on the bed while you stand up, pushing your strapped on member in and out between them, your own hands pressing them together as you work your widened hips into a rhythm.

I can see that she must lie down now, so that the feeling in her body can be completed—to feel her lady lover's cock between her tits, until they have burned the skin raw between the walls of flesh formed around it. I can see you in this impossible completion phase, my sister, fucking your cello teacher between her great tits, looking down at her, watching her hold on to your own great breasts from far below, watching her face anguish over with impossibility, as the pounding of your body against the bosom is the true source of these mysterious vibrations in her body, that send feelings that have already begun to grip her in her groin. You know instinctively, dear Angela, to pound her great bosoms as though trying to bring them harm, so careful not to allow yourself the privilege of a premature orgasm, lest this all important rhythm for the cello teacher be broken. So you close your eyes in anguish, dear Angela, so that your body will not tremble from the sight of this mature beauty's face and breasts underneath you. It is the closing of your eyes, dear Sister, the raising up of your lovely face to the Heavens that does the final trick for the cello teacher, as the waves from her breasts finally reach their destination, to where each pounding of your body against them rises the feeling in her groin higher and higher, until she must begin to whimper in fear for what is to come.

Now, open your eyes, dear Sister, so you many witness this miracle of nature, as the beautiful woman grips her great breasts for dear life upon a final, high pitch yelp, shocking in its intensity, amidst a look of pure pain on her face, as her head is thrown back, and she twists as if she is trying to roll out from underneath you. And it is the sight of her mysterious agony that grips your body at last, dear Angela, causing your hips to hit their involuntary stride of motion, until the lady cellists brief scream is answered by your own.

I can see the two of you in the bedroom of the luxury hotel, dear Angela, so far away from all prying eyes but your own, both staring unanswered into each other's eyes with determination, called, charged and commissioned to find every gemstone of breast pleasure you can, whether scattered about in plain sight, or mined from deep beneath the surface of desire.

Sunset Over Eden

The taste of forbidden fruit is sweet to the palate, and as bitter as wormwood in the soul. These are the depravities born from the tree of Eve, that lurk in the shadows of every secret place east of Eden, waiting for these unsuspecting souls to enslave.

The first bite of this profound disobedience rings like a chime in her ears, as the world around her become as a projection of dreams, where every blade of green grass, and the plush green leaf canopy of shading trees suddenly takes onto itself a mood less tranquil, as though its familiarity suddenly fills her with a spark of contempt.

I see the voluptuous, raven haired beauty of the garden, shaped in curviness like none that would be born after her, the profoundly heavy breasted, full hipped beauty in statuesque form—I see this woman look upon the glory of the fruit bitten and devoured, to see its allure transformed to ugliness in her heart, with a profundity of hatred never before felt, as every inch of her body is morphed to a feeling she has never imagined in the eons of tranquility, until this energy gathers in the center of her body, to make her drop the bitten fruit to the ground unawares, as she must fall to her knees, placing her hands on the ground to anchor herself for what forbidden pleasure must happen to her body.

And I see this woman reduced to a wailing, a weeping she is privileged to experience in solitude, as this call of the wild flows in high pitched loveliness from her lips, followed by a spasmodic trembling of her body previously unknown, as a completeness of feeling previously unseen, which gathers again in the center of her flesh, to explode to every muscle and bone in a wave of transcendent ecstasy forlorn. So far beyond what innocent pleasures having shared with her husband through the ages of Paradise, where suddenly the memory of him is corrupted, and the echo of his voice is muffled in the chambers of her mind. In the aftermath of her body's devastation, she endures the remainder of this trembling, until the waves of unendurability have made their rise and fall, and she may again return to sanity.

And in the haze of her soul's displeasure, in the fog of weary enlightenment, this beauty raises her head up from her gaze upon the forest floor, unaware of what new depth of sensuality burns from a hypnotic gaze, nor of what spark of awareness burdens her expression. I see this natural form, sitting in heavy, pendulous breasts upon the forest floor, her lovely hands clasped together in a shield over her features, leaned forward in feeble hiding, feeling tingles and twinges echo about her body and soul, with the knowledge that she has disobeyed the voice of God, and what Judgment he hath promised looms in the coming evening day.

And suddenly, she is aware that the dark and cunning presence she felt before has left the Garden in fear, terrified of his own epic accomplishment, and of what tragic consequences therein Creation must lie. I see a flash of wisdom unknown to the woman before descend in dread, as she stands in full beauty and somber refrain, looking down at her own two breasts exposed, seeing them as never before, feeling herself exposed in the light of the setting sun.

In the sunset over Eden, the shapely, statuesque woman draws another fruit from the forbidden tree, looking with disdain across the clearing, to where she knows she must go, to find the innocent Keeper of the Garden, to entice him to partake of the fruit whose taste on the tongue is sweet, but to the heart and soul are as bitter as wormwood.

Along this road of human depravity, I travel. Where every forbidden and secret thing passed down is grown and nurtured, fruits born from the Tree of Eve. From the Garden of Antiquity east of Eden. Along this road of earthen anomalies, the dark beauty of every twisted motivation revealed, I see the pain of the lady cellist revealed, and unleashed in softness and screaming upon the heart and mind of innocence, the body of her Asian student uncovered. Along this road of hidden depravities revealed, there is the woman of cultured civility, whom none would know beyond her sensual handling of the cello in public, and the shy, studious manner displayed over the years. None were aware of this breast goddess' breast obsession, her private self nursings, the filling of herself with her own breast milk many times over the years, the ability to bring herself to climax from this art alone. What private and unseen acts are passed down from the Tree of Eve, to torment the souls of hypocrisy to ruin?

Adelia Evanopoulos is somewhere above even a breast queen, above even the H-cupped Asian girl she was lucky enough to meet—whom she believed was a gift from God himself, sent to her to satisfy her own burning, tortured desire. Adelia is not a breast queen, which is not significant enough a description. Adelia is a *breast goddess*—in possession of the exotic Greek-Italian beauty in the face, above breasts pitched up to the unseen key of J for jubilee. A woman in possession of such a rare and special sensitivity, so that merely the squeezing of them is the prelude to ecstasy. I see the cultured, mature beauty in possession of this gift, finally able to secure a session in the bedroom of her home, in front of the bedroom mirror.

The woman is in paradise on Earth, being lucky, or blessed enough to have her young student naked behind her. Raising her heavy breasts up, up and up, letting them drop so heavily back into place. The pounding, flopping motion settles her nerves into another state of being, to where the serenity of feeling crosses over into arousal. She leans far back against her young student, feeling Angela Tao's own great breasts pushed against her back, to cushion this latest rise and fall.

I see the great breasted woman look down at the Asian girl's hands, lifting up her heavy bosom, glancing at the magnificent sight in the mirror, her entire body twitching a shudder when her student takes hold of the nipples and pinches them without ceasing. She must allow this word "yes" to come out on its own, along with the nodding of her head in a quiet, controlled desperation. Oh, what anomalies are grown and nurtured, in the soil of human depravity!

I see the beautiful lady cellist, in the bedroom of her grand, empty home, being serviced by the angel of her deepest longing, a busty beauty of Asian descent, dedicated to feeding her own breast obsession. The woman begins to writhe her bare hips against the Asian girl behind her, pressing her hand below her abdomen, just above her groin. Then, as if obeying her own inner thirst to be quenched, the Asian girl ceases the pulling and squeezing, moving to the side of the helpless breast goddess, to pull one of the great breasts deeply into her mouth.

I see Adelia lose her ability to exhale, or even to draw a breath at all, as she marvels at the wave of feeling flowing from her nipple to the rest of her body. The Asian girl sucks this nipple to the extreme erection, at last pulling away in the loud, sucking kiss, taking the nipple firmly in hand, beginning to jerk her hand rapidly at the front of Adelia's breast, pulling on the nipple in rapid rhythm, which shakes the great breast in mighty waves. This pulling, this shaking of her breast at the nipple immobilizes her further, until her body reminds her to breathe, followed by a slow moan of weeping intent, as the Asian girl jerks upon the nipple of her goddess without mercy.

Oh, what anomalies are nurtured and grown, in the soil of human depravity!

Angela Tao holds on tight to the breast goddess in secret, as the thick droplets of rare colostrum begin to drip from the nipple onto her hand, in awe of the sound of a grown woman's voice in weeping, and the feel of unseen energy that trembles every inch of the woman's body.

25

Woman is wayward is the song I hear, sung over the dreamy landscape of this latter day storm. A refrain important enough to be gathered up into the arms of the most popular operatic aria ever written, which flowed so freely from Verdi's pen. At the window of our country refuge, still marveling at the power and intensity of such a storm, I hear the aria from the impressive, old style speakers, booming and soaring though the house, a piece I had never heard in its entirety, in the sixteen years I floundered and wandered through this life. I listen to the Italian man sing *La donne e mobile,* reading in the liner notes earlier of its announcement to the world, that this is the mind of Eve passed down, and the full flowering of it is a sign of the times.

And what are these dreadful signs that are read, to warn us of the end of the age? The world is on the edge of the Second Coming, I fear, though all scoff and ridicule its possibility, where the Lord will return not in humility, but in glory. Where the Almighty himself will enact fiery revenge on the world for having rejected his love, through the sacrifice that was made on the cross at Calvary. For some reason, this burdens my heart and mind as the beautiful and terrible truth, that will encompass the life and death of humanity, and the soul of every human being who was ever born.

This world I see, this world I feel, this strange place 20 years in the making, where I am but a future girl, thrown here from the past—this world is on the edge of the Second Coming of Christ, as it is foretold by human behavior. Verdi's aria sings the last and greatest sign born from the hearts of men—it is the revelation of the established truth in secret, that woman is wayward indeed, and the proliferation, the revelation, the domination of female perversion is at hand. Where the prophecies of Christ will begin to convince people once and for all of what truth in prophecy the Holy Scriptures lay—*"Because iniquity shall abound, the love of many shall wax cold."*

And this is carried and supported by so many dark promises revealed, among which is the migration of the feminine mystique, where the woman is about to abandon the natural use of the man. The world is poised on the edge of Amazonia, where the spirit of female domination must spread like a pandemic, to keep the divorce court dockets filled to capacity. Female sexuality is the new mainstream, where James Cameron's heroin prophecies will be made known in our reality, and the spirit of the battle angel must soon come to light. *All of them witches,* is the message explored in the endtime, from the *ship shuba,* silly suburban nightmare of the Fourth Activity Paranormal, to the wickedly perverse fantasies of Stepford Wives and Rosemary, the new Stepford Wife is a suburban witch, holding her husband and her children captive in her spell, a prisoner of her emotional whim, where to be a bitchy-assed drama queen is a status symbol, and to hold the family in the dark heart of fear is a privilege to be desired.

Angela and me live in the invisible bars of this prison, having both been born into the heart of darkness, and raised by the unseen hand of female perversion and depravity. I wonder why I was spared the crossing over, why I was taken just before the conduit door was opened, and the spirit of what was passed into her would find its way into my mind and body. Of what strangeness this Ja'net Littledove spirit may be—I can feel it all over my sister when she is near me, and especially when we are engaged in the unspeakable. When she pins my arms to my sides, and slowly pounds herself into me in missionary, I can feel the spirit of sadism in repression, which causes her to press down onto me with as much heaviness as she can produce, as if trying to squeeze the breath out of me. It is where I can see the loveliness of her Asian features transformed to dark beauty, and a hidden ruthlessness that puts my nerves on a razor's edge.

I know that whatever negativity there is was placed there by Ja'net Littledove, born from their first session in the bedroom at the mirror, when the wooden ruler first introduced Angela's nipples to the truth about pain, and to Mother's body the truth about pleasure. I am worried a little, I think, when I perceive the strength of her biting at my breasts, or the heaviness of a swat at my buttocks, or the burning in my scalp when my blonde hair is pulled. I don't know if she is fully aware of where it is she is taking our intimacy, if she is aware that she is so completely accursed—a seven year molestation victim of a world renowned lady cellist, and a twenty year victim of beatings, scourges, bitings and blood from the rich woman who calls herself her mother.But even in the throes of our sickness, in the grips of what the world knows as forbidden, I can still sense an epic compassion she has for me, and a desire to see me achieve a recovery from the end of the world place I've been.

"Angela, please don't," I had said. *"I've got a bad feeling about this."*

"You've got a bad feeling? I haven't slept in two days."

"Then why are you doing this? I thought Mom said she didn't want anybody to know? What if she finds out you told?"

"By the time she finds out, maybe I'll have convinced her we have to tell the world about this. Its legitimate, Caley. It might be the most powerful thing that's ever happened to a human being. Its bigger than all of us...including Mom."

Jonathan Lovejoy

The Wade-Tao Principle

26

*T*amela Wade rides the rain and wind. Head of the dept of Physics and Astronomy in Charlottesville, at the big state university. Having been subject to the spirit of Eschatology. Unprepared for what it is that awaited her on the road to Woodland, at the house in the country. The house on the outskirts of Woodland Falls.

Tamela Wade rides the wind and rain. Black luxury SUV, protecting her from the storm. From the spirits of this end of the world thunder and lightning. Having walked face first into a magic that even she is unprepared for. Having climbed to the top of academia, by way of ethnicity patronized, hidden underneath yellow-skinned beauty and tan eyes, and hair as straight as it is long. Mother of two girls. Wife of a former professional athlete of a husband. Dark haired, handsome washout, safe in the arms of an engineering degree and a professional team on his resume.

Tamela Wade. Mother of two ivory skinned cuties. Cuties that have no beauty. None that she has ever been able to see. Daughters to be pushed. To be prodded. To be provoked. To be paddled. Daughters that cannot satisfy the grieving spirit within. Daughters she cannot be attracted to. Daughters she resents. Daughters she despises. Daughters she bears secret embarrassment for, because they are not as pretty. Because they smile and laugh in privilege, but not being among the brightest flowers in this garden of the successful. The garden of latter day hope. Where the pride of life is born and nurtured. Where the beautiful people go to live and die.

Tamela Wade. Princeton. Light skinned exotic. Daughter of a white woman. Daughter of the unspoken. The unspeakable.

Tamela Wade remembers the phonecall from Woodland Falls. Where Angela Tao convinced her over the phone that what she had to say was so extraordinary, so sacred, so special under the hidden sun, that she must drive this two hour commute to her home.

Tamela remembers the motivation for the drive. The craving to see the untenured Asian woman in her natural habitat. The craving to be in a situation that can only exist in a fantasy. To see if that fantasy can be made into a reality. To have Angela's blouse opened to her face. To have what she imagines exposed to her. To get her hands upon them. To give suck, and the greed of suckling upon them. To finally give herself the shaking of her dreams. Done with her mouth at the waters of Paradise. At the fountain of God's mercy upon her aching desire.

Tamela Wade rides the wind and rain. Remembering the rolling beauty of Angela Tao's property. More of a country estate, really. Beyond what she imagined for the Asian beauty. Feeling the spirits of luxury and privilege. Feeling a warning inside. Ignoring the crossing over to oblivion.

In the heart of her memory, Tamela Wade gets out of the luxury SUV in the storm. Hurrying through the accursed rain in sensual beauty. Nerdism left on the cutting room floor of her life. Sensuality embraced. Our Lady of the Hips. In wiggle and woggle of the upper thighs and buttocks. Princeton.

Our Lady of the Hips rings the chimes of her destiny. At long last, under the porch shelter, the door to paradise opens, and the product of her dreams emerges. The Asian flower. The lady cellist turned academic. All grades and Asian grinning. A history of GPA's too high for her to ignore, greeting her at the door. Specialist in planetary astronomy. Lecturer extraordinaire. PhD in Astronomy from this very school. A minor in music.

Angel Tao opens the door for her. For Miss Princeton. Wife of the professional athlete and automobile company engineer. Mother of two.

Tamela walks into the country home with Angela Tao. Wet from her journey. Coats and cuteness delivered to her hostess. All smiles and fungalooga. Blatant, inappropriate compliment given, concerning the Asian's beauty. The Asian's figure. A twinge to the center of her body. The center of her soul.

When the refreshments are refused. When the seats are taken. Tamela listens to the voice of the forbidden. The voice of the unbelievable. The voice of eschatology. The voice of madness.

Tamela takes the driver's license from Angela Tao. Looking upon it with vague curiosity. Unimpressed by the unadorned prettiness in blonde doll do. Forcing a compliment about the Asian's white sister. Refusing to acknowledge the racial diversity between them. *How can this blonde white girl be your sister*, is the question unasked. The answer unspoken.

Look at the date, the Asian professor says. *Look at the year it was issued...*

Read the number of the year, Miss Princeton. Read the issue date from last century. Process it. Use that keen, analytical mind, inherited from your black father. Put aside your skepticism and lust, inherited from your white mother.

Now, see the photograph taken. Look at the magazine. Look at the magazine the pretty blonde girl in the picture is holding. Look at the science magazine about the probe that died on the passing comet. This year, Miss Princeton.

Look at the blonde girl from the old license. Look at the blonde girl from the picture taken yesterday.

Is this a twin?

Why is this girl's picture on a fake license from last century*?*

Is this girl really your sister?

Yes, I have the same magazine in my office, you say. *If this picture is real, then who is the girl in this 20 year old license,* you say.

Tamela is suddenly dim. Her wits dull from lack of understanding. The truth of her education exposed. No trekkie. No trekker. No true feel for the Einsteinian mind. For the dreams of Sagan. For first contact.

Tamela Wade looks up from the driver's license and the photograph. Taken 20 years apart. Taken a few days apart.

Tamela looks up from the bewilderment of twins, to their sister in triplicate standing before her.

A greeting. A smile. The pitiful question, *is this your sister?*

Now, the frustrated denouncement. Anger allowed, to protect yourself. Wondering why you drove two hours west, to the foot of the Blue Ridge Mountains, to see an untenured professor's sister in two pictures you don't understand. Pictures that expose you. Your dim wittedness. Your stubbornness. Your unbelief.

Now, read the newspaper clipping from a score of years. From two decades of journeys, from twenty trips of this doomed planet around the sun. Gauge the date of the article, Miss Princeton. Look closely at the name of the girl who is missing in the article, Miss Princeton. Look at the grainy, black and white photograph, Miss Princeton.

The rose upon your cheeks is the rage of hypocrisy. The surface of cultured civility. You were her best friend a moment ago, where you not? You wanted to drink the milk from her Asian tits a moment ago, did you not? Now, what do you want from her, Miss Princeton? A pound of flesh? A stream of blood? Why is your love transformed to hatred, Miss Princeton?

Did you have another sister who went missing 20 years ago? Another sister who looks just like her?

Now listen, Miss Hips. Miss Yellow-Skinned Beauty. Miss Trophy Wife. Miss Figure Head of the Department. Listen to the blonde ghost speak. Listen to Einstein's theory, of quick journeys taken by the unfortunate traveler at inter dimensional speed. Listen to the greatest scientific discovery of all time pour forth in nighttime vision: of forests, roads, and oceans in the dark of night. Listen to the terror of the Wade Tao Principle. The theory of the modern day.

Another twenty years of research. The descent of the world upon the Road to Woodland.

Tamela Wade rides the wind and rain. Away from the country estate. Away from the house at Woodland Falls. Deciding already in your heart what must be done. Desperate to get home. To call your colleagues, and relate the story from the first word to the last. To accuse the Asian of trickery. Of deceit. Of trying to bring you in upon a ridiculous hoax to the scientific world. Devising a scheme with end of the world audacity.

Tamela is in grieving to tell. To lay the groundwork for a rapid suspension. The foundation for a rapid dismissal. To turn her back on the Asian bitch. After making her believe you were going to help her. That you would start the snowball down the hill.

Along the road to Woodland east, so far to Charlottesville in the storm. Tamela's heart is zapped in fear, from the flash of lightning into the woods in front. The blast of sound it makes.

Tamela cannot see the collapse of her world, in the felling of a giant tree across the highway. Tamela does not feel the agony of truth, the curse of mankind befallen, when the tree crashes so heavy across the roof of her SUV in the road. The crushing of a life out of existence. The shattering of glass and steel.

The splattering of bone and blood.

What collective jade hoax is this?

These are the words that wake me up with a start in the middle of the night—a half day's removal from the coming and going of Tamela Wade. Words I hear spoken as clear as a bell in the air around me, in the voice I remember as hers. Angela wakes up beside me, as if startled awake by my sudden revelation of things to come.

"What is it, Caley?"

"She doesn't believe you."

"Who, Tamela?"

"I just heard her call it a "jade hoax.""

"Of course she believes us. You saw her. You know she did."

Angela reaches out to where I sit bolt upright in the bed, gripping me around the waist in half sleep, pulling me over to her. I lie down beside her, facing away in this wee hour spooning, listening to her breathing tell me that she has already fallen asleep again.

The raised pounding of my heart in my chest is the companion of something close to fear in my body. I am suddenly aware of a dark, mocking presence in the room, making me more than glad for the presence of my sister in this storm.

She keeps the demons away
She holds the demons at bay
In the rain where ghosts and shadows play
Is the pain of every price we pay

My nerves are ripped to shreds by the loud, pseudo-chimes of G and E chords, so rudely spat out by Angela's phone on the night stand. The professor rolls over to answer whatever strange calling this is in the middle of the night, already having been startled wide awake by me.

Let the little rectangular, Star Trek flip thing that dares inhabit space as an actual phone ring until its done, dear Angela? Hit the ring killing button, and roll back over here to me, Dear Angela? No. This time, a middle of the night call must be answered, in all its end of the world implications, and glory.

Answer the phone, dear Angela. Hear what message flies about me, from the mind of Miss Princeton to thee. Answer the tolling of the bells, dear Angela. Find out for whom the bell tolls. It tolls for thee.

"Hello? Yes, I'm Angela Tao. An accident? Yes, I know her quite well, she was just here today... actually, she told me her husband and her

119

two daughters had gone to visit his parents… he'll probably check his messages by tomorrow morning…okay, I'll be there as soon as I can."

Angela flips the little phone thing closed, already an anachronism in the age of technology. Already, I can see that she refuses to be burdened by confusion, to be held down by false innocence about what must be.

"I hope she's alright," she says.

Knowingly.

28

Angela and I ride the nighttime streets of this town. Hardly able to see beyond the hood of our luxury ride in the dark, as the raindrops of warning are gathered in front of us to infinity. The windshield wipers are hopeless in their desperation, unable to give more than the briefest glimpse of clarity in the country dark. These stretches of rural highway are treacherous enough in the tranquility of sunlight, let alone the ominous miles of nighttime foreboding, where the drowning rainfall seeks to make them impassable in the storm. The reasons for this trip are so painfully obvious to the both of us, having been heightened to a greater awareness of cause and effect, a greater knowledge of the tragedy of human existence, which is Fate.

What pressures there are that ebb and flow naturally in a human life—these are they which have gripped the two of us in knowing, as when stepping out of a warm house into the deadly cold of winter, and being gripped by the truth down to the marrow of bone. Both of us were aware this afternoon that we were in the garden of thistles, where the gathering of every rose flower is a pricking of our skin to blood. And this blood is mingled with the blood of another on our hands, as we traverse the miles of nighttime wind and rain, to the hospital bed where the woman of corporate looks and learning is laid.

Neither of us can say a word toward the welfare of Tamela Wade, lest it cause a painful surfacing of this bizarre truth we know. But still, the questions haunt our minds and bodies—they haunt the air around us in spirit form, until Angela sees me raise my hand to my lips in a visible tremble, and turn to gaze pitifully at the rainy driver's side window. Angela reaches over to take my hand away from my lips, and holds on tight as she continues to drive. In the eerie glow of the nighttime lights and numbers inside our car, I am again comforted by the presence of my big sister, who is my little sister now all grown up, as she protects me from the menacing powers and principalities that flow.

The dark, forest road reminds me of the dark road once again, where I saw the trees give place to that mysterious nighttime ocean, which seemed to stretch outward toward the stars that glowed, outward to an earthen infinity. The memory is a flash of trauma, making me grip my sister's hand tighter, wishing I could move closer to her as she drives. Among this flash of trauma flows the voice of a scream I remember, when our mother escorted Angela into the kitchen out of my sight.

Along the flow of our time and history, I am burdened by the knowledge and revelation of truth, seeing my mother's beautiful, bitter expression on the nighttime road to Woodland, driving her eighteen year old daughter home from a local recital, where she saw her perform her Rossinian magic on the cello in the form of a teardrop, *Une Larme,* born from the composer's *Péchés de vieillesse,* his Sins of Old Age, left for future generations to see.

While the tragicomic strands of this bygone melody are spoken by the cello teacher turned piano accompanyist, and her lovely immolation (victim) upon the pre-professional cello string, I see Mother in their fungalooga walk through the parking lot afterwards, in the cold of a frosty November night, underneath the Forest Moon.

As the slow part of this melody plays in comic sadness, in mock tragedy for what is to come, I see the sophisticated blonde woman, I see Mother tell my sister in her ear—"get in the back seat," enjoying her eighteen year old daughter's bewilderment as they slide into the back seat of black Cadillac luxury. In the local theater parking lot, I see the woman slide tall and strong in the back seat up against her daughter. Hearing her whisper these words in secret:

Who the Hell do you and that Greek bitch think you are? Hmm? Look at me.

As we drive the dark, rainy miles, the fear and pain of Angela's life reaches out to the theater of my mind, showing me the woman in the dark'ned back seat of the car, with her face hardly an inch away from her daughter's.

She wants to fuck you.

And what does this comment do for you, my sister? Among the types of fear there are, what cold, icy hand is this which grips your soul?

Does she make you open your blouse when you play? Does she make you play in your bra? Listen to me, and listen good. You and that Greek cello bitch together on stage don't mean a damned thing to me. Don't you ever think that this makes you independent from me. I am your mother. Do you understand that?

I hear the words *Yes, Ma'am* leap out on their own, my sister. In hopes that a splash of water thrown quick enough will quench the flames of this fire.

When we get home, Mother says, *you're going to take your top off. And I'm going to twist both your nipples and listen to you scream.*

Mother takes her daughter's lovely face by the chin. Staring into her daughter's eyes. Into your eyes, Angela.

I'm going to do it, until it makes me cum.

In the closed space of Cadillac luxury, there rings the most massive face slap imaginable. I see the woman raise her hand at you, and bring it across your face in full violence. Watching you stare. Knowing you are too afraid to move. Watching the teardrop flow down your face when you blink.

29

I blink to clear my vision, as we approach the brightly lit part of the rainy highway. Shimmering through the windshield as we slow down are the colors of danger, painted orange and yellow on the machines, and lit up in the lights that form arrows pointing, and in the lighted words CAUTION: SLOW AHEAD. Through the rain soaked windshield and passenger windows, all of this is bathed in the ambient light of earthly progression, glowing white over the entire eerie scene, illuminating the men of a late night emergency crew dispatched, finally having cleared the highway of what we see on the side of the road, which are the remains of one of the tallest and thickest trees in these woods, the huge trunk cut into three massive sections, the bottom section to the left of our car as we creep by in the storm.

Angela rolls the window down in bewilderment, that we both may get a better view of the splintered tree stump at the edge of the woods, and the section of splintered trunk fallen from it. To the right of the broken glass covered highway are the other two sections of this massive tree, with chainsaws just beginning their angry screams into the surrounding storm, about to make work of the deadly branches where they lay. The sight of such a large tree fallen is as unnerving as it is unnatural, infusing the whole section of highway with otherworldliness, and an aura of foreboding and dread.

And parked nearby the fallen tree, and the cluster and clutter of lights and machines is a tow truck with its orange light flashing on top, with something hooked up to the back of it and raised to an angle, to reveal that it was once some kind of a vehicle, before the hood and roof of it was crushed downward into oblivion. The middle tree section's handiwork, to be sure, stretched across the top of this vehicle for an impossibly long time, even after it had been lifted just enough, so that the jaws of life could get to what was left of the person inside. And then there were more hours passed in the storm, until at last the great pine was moved off the highway, and then the smashed remains of earthen luxury. All of this, in the grip of a powerful storm, where gale force winds blow with alarming frequency, and every spark of lightning carries with it a warning of things to come.

We roll onward, past the chaos of yesterday and today, moving toward what awaits us further down the road, the impending chaos of tomorrow. Angela takes so much time rolling up her window, that I almost let it slip that I know. But after another long moment of shock and awe, she finally rolls her window back into place, sheltering us again from the nighttime rain and wind.

We roll the last darkened miles of this storm, until the lights of Woodland Memorial beckon our horizon. These are the lights of earthly progression again, our amaranthine guide to safety and security, so intrinsically linked to the lights of what tragic chaos it was we were just passing through. We roll in silver Sonata luxury under the red letters glowing *Emergency,* parking close to the curb near the lighted doors of this obsession.

Our arrival under this great shelter is greeted by an infinity of rainfall all around us, falling in visible streams of fury, illuminated by the lights around the parking lot that glow. We both hurry across the smooth concrete, trying to get away from the heaviest rainfall either of us have ever seen, opening the magic doors in rapid escape from the nighttime storm.

Tamela Wade is the name I hear the Asian beauty speak to the nurse in tragic plainness, who seems to have already known that we were coming. We wait while she pages the doctor, calling him to the front desk to meet us, to escort us to the patient's room.

Its not long before the short, friendly man appears through the swinging doors where we are, in sort of a waddling motion, and a pleasant, kind-faced manner that rescues us from being ill at ease. But we notice that what kindness there is in his eyes, what pleasant look there may be in his expression is laced with the solemnity of deep compassion, and the need to be a comfort in the face of tragedy. The two of us stand helpless in the blast of arctic wind, which fills both our souls with winter. The two of us are stunned to silence as we walk, our words being held captive in our throats as we follow him down the hall, turning the corner into the room where the truth lies in repose, covered respectfully from head to toe in white linen.

All I can do is grab Angela's hand as we follow the doctor over to the bed, where he takes the sheet in hand, and moves it down and away from the face of what lies beneath. What we see underneath the covering touches the fear already imprinted inside, causing it to expand until the world around us is suddenly a wasteland, a wilderness of icy hopelessness and cold, bitter regret.

The two of us stand in awe of the face of beauty. The face of lifelessness. The face of death.

Witch's Crown

30

Mother Daughter Perversion

Has become a thing of beauty to see

An end of the world diversion

On the eve of eschatology

31

Mother daughter perversion is pervasive. It is the great secret that has held us captive for centuries. This, not just the 'us' of present company, but humanity as a whole, Women who think nothing of sticking their tongues in their twelve year old daughter's mouths, of having their daughters stick their fingers inside their big bottom in the soapy shower bath. These woman have discovered this secret doorway to the most powerful orgasms that a woman can have. A real orgasm, which is devastation to her body, either in noise or silence, that devastates her senses for a moment, where she can hardly remember her name. It is a secret that becomes a drug to these women, until they become predatory, holding their daughters captive to this perversion for many years, sometimes form early childhood far into adulthood. And the energy it produces swings both ways along this unique river that flows, infusing the daughters with this self same craving, until they understand that no man, no woman, no vibrator machine—nothing will ever explode the dynamite into their bodies like their mother can. The cure for what ails these women can only happen through the sharing of this secret, through the passing down of it to their own daughter—be it an adopted or foster child, a niece, a child in their temporary custody or care, or God forbid, the queen of contact, the birth daughter herself, which has the power of ignition, where sometimes the women who have been attempting a quiet quickie upstairs while Daddy is downstairs have been gripped with something that shot a sound out of their mouths they had never thought possible, where there is only left a desperate prayer that Daddy didn't hear it, with explanations ready and waiting in case he asks *what in God's name was that noise...*

Your daughter snuck up behind me and scared the bejesus out of me, she'll say, *I want you to talk to her about that, she's gonna give me a heart attack...*

The Mother learns the power of the Witch's Crown in all its forms, orgasms that are achieve through benign stimulation, where hardly a motion is necessary beyond a deep kissing, or nipples rubbed together, or a light spanking, or bottoms pressed and bounced together, or even whatever kamasutric positions they discover, where no movement or full nudity is necessary—the mother's voice will wail the tell tale siren into the walls of their secret room. It is a secret so pervasive as to be epidemic, a disease that has grown to pandemic proportions, spreading like a cancer underneath the surface of cultured civility.

The Road to Woodland

This is our last and greatest trauma. The last great revelation before the endtime, before the untold millions of souls are disappeared into nothingness, as the eve of the Second Coming of Christ unfurls. It is the last and greatest glimpse into the heart of the darkness that is the human soul, the depravity that opens the possibilities for Holocausts of every kind, when children are drawn into the history books in shock and disbelief, when they read of trainloads of Jews being herded off to Auschwitz, when they read of the shiploads of Africans captured and set sail for North America, when they see the photographs of the slaves with backs scarred beyond recognition, these are glimpses into the depravities of the human soul...

When credit scores have become the measure of human worth in the modern civilization. When houses are foreclosed upon, and families are thrown helpless into the streets of their town. When the 35th of 36 payments of a car is missed, and the repossession men are sent as thieves in the night. When a twenty year customer of a cable company is cut off from the sanity of their latter day entertainment, because the company refuses the arrangement to help the customer through hard economic times. When the homeless wander the streets in disillusionment and despair. These are glimpses into the evil heart that is mankind.

When parents imprison and rape a little girl so badly that her genitals are damaged from the trauma. When books of crazy mothers who torture their children are *fact* and not fiction. When books of crazy women who burn the genitalia of a teenage girl are *fact,* and not fiction. These are glimpses into the heart of darkness that we know. These are signs of the times. When privileged mothers gather their children for a bath, then drown them like lost souls in a flood. When privileged mothers gather their children for bed, then cut their innocent white skin to blood. When privileged mothers gather their children in a car, to roll them into drowning waters through the mud. When children look to their mothers, to wonder where it is that they go. These are signs of the times.

32

*H*er eyes were open.

The doctor's apology, and his embarrassed brushing of Tamela Wade's open eyes closed is the scene I am plagued with now, as I am gripped in the throes of a weeping fit outside the hospital. The driving rain cascades a crystal waterfall all around us. Bestowing a curtain of falling water from the shelter to the ground. From these tears of falling sky I hear, to the ones that tickle my crying eye, there is the tragedy of revelation to fear.

"Of *course* its my fault," I say, hugging her tight and unashamed, as the people who wander in and out are briefly mesmerized by the sight of a blonde teenage girl sobbing in the arms of an Asian beauty.

"Look at me," she says, pulling my head back from her shoulder by the hair. "Don't you *ever* let me hear you say that again."

"But its *true*, Angela," I say, "The way Mom threatened you the other day and now this. She died because you *told*. She died because you *told.*"

The last syllable reduces me to another fit of weeping, leaning against her shoulder again, so glad for the feel of her great bosoms against me, and her strong hands caressing my back. After another long moment has passed, when this wave of sobbing flows through, she ushers me away from the hospital doors to our silver luxury, placing me safely inside. I watch the strong bodied, beautiful Asian woman bounce gracefully through the rain to the driver's side door, getting inside as quickly as she can, being somehow made more beautiful by the storm's attack on her. I watch her take a deep breath and rub her hands back through her hair in sleepy frustration, amazed at the sight of this exotic woman so close to the touch, who is so concerned with my health and well being. I see nothing of the funny face little Asian girl I left behind, as I watch God form a real time snapshot of his handiwork to me, as she holds her deep breath with her hands behind her head for a long moment, her eyes closed, her head tilted back, her magnificent breasts pushed forward gigantic and rounded, under a face so deeply Asian and beautiful. This pose she strikes without knowledge or effort, done just for me by Fate, that I may witness her as one of the most physically beautiful women in the world.

Angela exhales this elegant breath, moving her hand gracefully over to my blonde hair, stroking it once, then holding the back of my head while she leans over and presses her lips so firmly to mine without apology, moaning a little, to vibrate my hopeless body to awareness, and my helpless soul to oblivion.

"Are you alright?" she says, mint breath in my nostrils, making me shake my head yes in the manner of a sad little girl being comforted by her mother. My thirty two year old sister is, biologically, old enough to be my mother as it is, and sometimes, I can feel the nature of our dynamic in the throes of this quantum shift, where I am beginning to feel as though I have been pulled from the womb of another, and thrown onto her doorstep to be found and cared for.

The cranking of the engine transports me to the car of her youth, and hands of suburban beauty on the keys of Cadillac luxury. The woman turns the car off and tells her daughter, *"go upstairs and take off every stitch of your clothes. In my room."*

The *"yes Maam"* is apt to come out on its own, as it is often so inclined to do. I see the Asian girl from so many years ago, so far from the mature, sensual beauty that she will become, though her young breasts already carry the heft of generations, and bear the extraordinary weight of their calling. I see this young Asian beauty obediently step out of their car in the approaching Virginia night, in the faded light of the evening day, waving to the blonde ponytailed dog walker who shows herself to the neighborhood in skinny-prettiness every evening. The wave flashes false hope to her spirit, and she speaks of gathering her cello from the back and taking it into the house, answered by the reminder of her condemned place in the world:

"Get your ass upstairs. Now."

The Asian girl is shocked back to a reality she had tried to forget. Trying once again to hide behind the cello, hoping that her mother seeing her dragging the heavy thing into the house would evoke sympathy. But in the two year history of this tragedy, she cannot remember a shred nor strand of compassion from the rich woman, whom everyone knows as the friendliest, prettiest of the charity queens, and could not fathom such a manner and degree of this behind closed doors cruelty.

In the shadow of the evening day, the daughter casts one more fleeting glance to the leading edge of infinity, the few bright stars that have begun to decorate the sky around the crescent moon. And against her better judgment, she glimpses the woman in Cadillac luxury in the black asphalt driveway, watching her sit comfortably in her driver's seat, staring her dead in the eye. The daughter moves upon this spark of fear, opens the door to her Woodland Falls estate, and disappears inside.

Insolent little cunt, are the words that torment the Angela Littledove mind while she goes up the stairs, cursing her workaholic, absentee father for always being out of town, blaming him so briefly in her heart for not knowing about his wife's sickness, and what it projects through her onto his daughter's mind body and spirit. But thoughts of him dissipate upon the sound of the door being opened behind her, as she takes the last few steps at the top of the stairs, rounding the corner quickly, hurriedly into the hall, and to the door of their tragedy's upper room. She reaches back to the top of the zipper on her dress, undoing it in part, then reaches around again, unzipping it the rest of the way. Crisscrossed among the thick, white bra straps is a network of angry scars, some ghostly, and some with life but from a few days ago.

The daughter hurries out of her dress and her shoes, her stockings, and then her bra and underwear, still unable to get used to the impossible size and hanging, bulbous shape of what her bra has abandoned. She stands in front of the mirror exposed, crossing her arms in front of the great bosoms, staring at the deeply curved waist and widened hips, hearing nothing of the quality they possess from her own mind, but only the words "fat breasted bitch" spoken over and over again.

A tingle at the covered nipple twinges upon the clicking of the door, and the unnerving entrance of her mother.

"Mother?" A pleading cry for mercy.

Unheard.

"Mother, please tell me what I did wrong. Tell me, and I swear to God I won't do it again. Mother, I swear it."

Inside the huge closet, the frustrated woman suppresses a deeper frown, removing her shoes and placing them on the floor, on the bottom of the thirty eight other pair, which all seem to her a product of necessity rather than vanity.

"Mother?"

"Shut up," the woman snaps, genuinely unable to endure the sound of her daughter's voice again.

"But if you'll just tell me what I did, so I won't do it again? Please?"

Inside the Ja'net Littledove mind, the woman feels the ire ignite the Curlingale blood. Unable to even consider not doing so, she walks out of the closet in stocking foot. Determination, walking quickly over to the naked Asian girl at the mirror.

"Turn around," she says. *"Face me. Put your arms down, hold them behind your back."*

In the wake of this compliance, is born the pain she cannot grow accustomed to, as the woman grabs and twists both nipples without mercy, as if tuning the sounds her daughter makes throughout the twisting.

"Oh, yeah. That's the sound your cello teacher wants to hear you make, isn't it? Hmm? I said put your hands down, bitch."

There is no going back through time, dear daughter. There is no stepping backward along the timeline, to avoid this misstep, to avoid having spoken out of turn, to avoid the pain of this fire in your bosom. In the knowledge of this, in the profoundest regret for days of living, she clasps her hands behind her back with as much strength as she can conjure up, hearing the sound of her own voice escape again into the room. The mother holds her daughter's breasts still, watching the independence, the insolence fade, amidst the return of hopelessness, and submission to the dominant will. The mother holds them there, not from any idea of mercy her daughter may receive, but that a third twist of her daughter's nipples would most likely send her own body into a premature oblivion.

Unbuttoning her tight, silken gray blouse, the woman walks in renewed energy back to the closet of dreams, this walk into a cavern of feminine desire gone epic, which is truly the size of a small room. She reemerges with the belt they both know so well, tossing it to the bed, removing her gray blouse and navy skirt with its subtle, matching gray pattern woven in, to remind every spirit voyeur that the width of her hips is very nearly as extraordinary as the size of her daughter's breasts. A set of *horizon hips*, if such a thing exists, to explore in full the possibilities of small-waisted, wide-hipped femininity.

The white woman with the bubble and spread leaves her small, black underwear on, to cover so skillfully the front of her in bikini fashion, to frame the shape of woman to its full, hourglass glory. She picks up the belt and walks over to her naked young victim, *whacking* the belt down to her daughter's right nipple, then again after the grimace and flinch twice more, until her daughter breaks on the fourth swat with the belt across her nipple, screaming an erupting siren into the room.

"There she is," the mother says. *"The cello teacher's little Asian slut."*

The mother folds her belt in classic form, and proceeds to whip both her daughter's breasts with uncompromising harness, listening to her daughter struggle to have enough breath to fully scream, watching her daughter's tits wiggle with every blow, developing a network of pink welts striped across the big white of them. She finds herself unable to stop, unable to keep her promise to get behind her daughter, and twist both her nipples until her own body shakes to agony and grieving.

"Turn your ass around," she says. This, the daughter does, turning her own bubbly bottom to her mother, hardly able to see her own reflection now through the new flow of tears she shed. The next instant brings the fire to her naked buttocks, concentrated across the full width of them, the height, the depth and the breadth of them, completely below her daughter's scarred back, and above the scars of her upper thighs. The mother endeavors to bring herself to her proper place with this motion, striking her daughter's bottom with the fullest, hardest blows she is capable of, done in rapid succession, until she knows that she must stand against her daughter's backside, and feel the suffering before it is too late.

Through the whirlwind of her daughter's sobs and angry weeping, the woman presses herself against her daughter's bruised and welted bottom, inspired to pull the belt across both her daughter's breasts in full, strapping them immobile across both nipples now covered with the black leather, causing both gigantic tits to pop up above and below the belt held in place like a strap, showing the mother in the mirror something she had not yet considered in two years of this depravity. The sight of her daughter's Olympian breast flesh bulged around the strap pulled tight as a harness triggers a lightning bolt straight to her groin, causing her to scream in triplet, three high pitched soprano notes from Antiquity, each one louder than every scream her daughter had just delivered, her hips jerking forward as if on their own, by an explosion of energy that was nearly too great to bear, which had caused the screams in triplet in part— screams born as much from shock and fear as they were from pleasure and pain.

The daughter watches her own reflection, marveling at the gigantic breasts bound by the belt across the front of them, the strength and trembling in her mother's body, and the memory of a sound that she had never heard her mother make before, as if she had touched the burning surface of something that was too hot for her body to endure.

Future Girl

33

She rides in beauty like the night. This breast obsessed woman who is my sister, burdened with a craving for pleasure in her own, and now, a taste for the pulling of mine into her pretty mouth. But what course in life is there left for her to have taken, being trapped in her own shrinking room like the rest of us, where there is only one window through which to escape, having been trained by her own mother in private, to appreciate the full spectrum of sensations placed upon them. Having been trained by her breast obsessed cello teacher, herself a breast goddess, focused and dedicated to the extremes of pleasure dispensed through the kissing, the licking, sucking and stroking of every inch of them, until her own Witch's Crown is achieved. I have been pulled out of time, and thrust in the midst of this rarity, in the midst of these breast queens, to observe and record their aberrant behavior, and its role as endtime prophecy. The remarkable behavior of these women, mothers, cello teachers and the like, presages and foretells the end of the age, when humanity will soon be at a place beyond redemption.

We ride onward from the hospital in the accursed pre-morning dark, accursed victims of such end of the world fascination passed down, un-innocent, writhing in the jaws of Fate, and what curses are passed down through the timeline. The death of Tamela Wade presses heavy on our spirits, a tragedy revisited in full understanding now on the road back to our country house, when we pass the remains of the fallen tree in the road. In the rising gray of dawn's early light, the scene is no less dramatic, infusing the waking world with the ghostly, phantasmal hue of legend, filling us with apprehension as we drive slowly by. The coming daylight is a tragic revelation, a reminder to us that we are both held prisoners of whatever it is that I am, and the both of us are now terrified of the idea of anywhere near the world stage, being received, ridiculed and rejected as Future Girl, teller of bald face lies, and her Asian professor friend, expecting them to believe these reports of the impossible. It is as though a barrier has been raised, a wall between me and the rest of the world, where I must be content with my own recovery, and what care my elegant and beautiful sister can provide.

We brave the rainy miles through the country without incident, until the elegance and beauty of our country home appears. The drive down the long, asphalt drive is pristine, even in the storm, where the spirits of country tranquility still move about, obeying the limits of their calling. Luck has no morality, and regardless of what behind closed doors secrets these good luck angels are privy to, they are charged by Fate to keep the dark spirits at bay, to protect the well-to-do in their hour of iniquity.

As we approach the lovely brick home, whose elegance is perceived shimmering through our windshield, the truth of Tamela Wade's sudden departure *hits* home, and I know that I cannot mourn another hour for the sophisticated lady of learning, as the chastity between her life and ours grows exponentially, to where Angela can never admit that her greatest regret about the *fake bitch's death* is that she never got a chance to *fuck her in the ass with a strapon.* This is the vulgar revelation of truth I bear, as we disembark our rainy chariot, and hurry through the storm into the front of the house.

Umbrellas quickly done away with, Angela takes me by the hand and guides me over to the sofa. As she sits down, with me standing up in front of her, I can feel that she is done with any pretense that may be left about us, and is ready once and for all to express the tragedy of her inner self in private. As it always is when she approaches me, my body is racked with nerves every bit as much as desire. I know she can sense this, as she unbuttons my sky blue collar shirt and slides it off. And I know that when she pulls my powder blue T-shirt out of my jeans and pulls it up over my bra, I know that I cannot hide from her what has amounted to the spirit of pure fear in my body.

And this, I can tell has arisen her profoundest need, that must be satisfied through the training of the cellist, the spirit passed onto her from the Evanopoulos mind. She raises my bra up from my breasts, gazing intently at the melody pitched in C minor, taking them both in her hands and massaging them gently, staring at the nipples, watching the areolas puff outward in the squeezing, at last, rubbing her nose and lips against my right breast, which sends a feeling into me that I can only describe as epic expansion.

The fear in me will not subside, even when she gently pulls the nipple into her mouth for one suck and release, the sum total of which makes me feel as though I may seriously piss my pants. Another long, sucking pull to the same nipple brings this feeling back again, causing me to wonder what dark magic can it be, that such a light touch pushes so heavy upon my bladder and groin.

She engages the nipple fully, sucking it as if there were milk to be had, until I can no longer fight the principality in my flesh, which strikes a spark to my groin that grows, causing my lungs to expand and contract on their own, spreading eventually to my voice, yelping a high pitched yip into the space around us.

I imagine the look on my face is the pain of shock and humiliation, which she drinks in through her lovely gaze, pulling me closer to her, leaving her head against my naked bosom, to feel me suffer another humiliating twitch and spasm. I am overwhelmed with amazement, the involuntary nature of what just happened to my body, and the explosive power of raw pleasure I endured. The quick, high pitched shriek had literally happened on its own accord, as I had tried with all my strength not to make a sound.

Angela holds me tight, listening to me regain control of my breathing, while she perceives an end of the world message in the storm.

he heights and depths of my mother's depravity are not lost on her, whether or not she is aware of it. What she does to us next, I don't know if it is deviant lovemaking or deviant love, if deviance at all can be garnered from it. Angela coaxes me down into her lap, laying with my head at her bosom. She pulls her black T-Shirt up over her bra, which I see from down below, like a traveler at the base of a mountain hill. She tells me to take her breast out, the one nearest my head, which I clumsily struggle to do while she watches me.

Angela's nipples are naturally erect, with large, brown areolae in perfect circles, that shrink and wrinkle greatly when she is aroused, pushing her nipples out twice as far as normal. I notice that these huge areola are perfectly smooth and unshrunken as of yet, and something inside me knows that the sign of their full arousal is pending.

When the great, fleshy breast is pulled out of the bra, she takes it into her hand, and guides it into my waiting mouth. What comfort there is to be garnered, I can feel flowing through to my entire body, as I lay in her lap with my own breasts covered, with her nipple pulled into my mouth like a suckling child. I stare up at her once, watching her look down at me as a mother would, in loving curiosity, stroking my hair away from my face once, refusing to look away. I draw a mother's comfort from my sister's bosom, nursing deeply upon the nipple without ceasing, watching her at last have to close her eyes and hold her head back calmly, to savor the continuous wave of pleasure that flows through.

As to what deviance this may appear to be, a sixteen year old blonde girl nursing at a 32 year old Asian woman's heavy breast, this, I choose not to know as it applies to me, as the pleasure and comfort I am receiving from it is simply too great for me to resist. The stroking of her hand so gently on my face, the caress of her other hand on my leg, serve to lift and carry me to a place of bliss, where I am aware of her deep and heavy breathing.

It is the heart of her soul's memory we feel, when she is a young girl of eighteen, on Sunday afternoon after church service, locked in her bedroom with our mother. Mother is in full church lady attire, complete with her blouse of the deepest burgundy cloth, unbuttoned and opened with her nursing bra secretly bought and worn, where the nursing flap of one cup is folded open, while her eighteen year old daughter is laid across her lap in the locked room, while the father visits and laughs with others in their Sunday afternoon football foolishness.

Ja'net Littledove stares down at her daughter, running her gaze up and down every inch of her, her face twisted in awe and disbelief at what sight this is, and the feel of her grown daughter sucking at her breast like a child. The sound of foolishness downstairs begins to haze into nothing in the woman's hearing, as every pull of the nipple into her daughter's mouth begins to pull energy up from her groin, until it traverses the distance up to the nipple being suckled. The daughter opens her eyes to the sight of this fully dressed, sophisticated woman with the look of madness in her expression, her mouth hung open in a phantom scream, condemned to be held in, whose energy is diverted to every corner of her trembling body. The look in the woman's eyes is one of pleading, as speech is no longer possible, and the grip of her sanity is briefly lost...

At the onset of my sister's trembling, I look up at her in time to see the same madness in her eyes, and the devastation of defeat washed over her awestruck expression.

The

Earthquake Game

35

*T*amela Lippincott was her name. When her mother used to play the Earthquake Game. Even in spite of the years of Laura Lippincott's cruelty, there was always a doorway left unblocked, a window to this left open, so that her little yellow skinned beauty of a daughter and she could sneak and play this game, which commenced only in the bathroom, and only when they were completely alone in the house. And little twelve year old Tamela understands that this secret is locked down and pressurized from Joe Lippincott, Mr. Twelve Hour A Day Blue Collar King, all black muscles and a smile white enough to have gathered up this assy white queen for the upper lower class ride.

He works hard for the money, Mr. Forklift by day, Don Juan button pusher in a factory part time by night. Seven o'clock in the morning to eight o'clock at night, the ghost of Joe Lippincott hovers unseen, in the little white working class house by the streets of Davidson County. This bored and lonely white woman, cursed with a life she had never thought possible for someone as pretty as herself, doubly cursed with a little yellow child she hardly even knew.

Laura Lippincott hardly knows this smart little straight A student, still in the sixth grade, driven to straight A's by the strict father, who has charged the mother with *"whipping her little yellow ass black and blue,"* whenever she brings home a grade lower than a B. *"I think you should let me beat her ass for the B's too,"* Laura would say, but to no avail. There was enough pressure and opportunity as it is, to keep her understanding that, let alone the report cards, a "C" on any test was grounds for a whipping from her mother, which Joe Lippincott would sometimes witness, if he were not trapped on the clock in one of his factories or warehouses, where overtime is a prison beyond iron bars, to a dark'ned door in a solitary dungeon. Sixty to eighty hours a week hard labour, young Tamela's father was accustomed to, so that Laura Lippincott was sorely neglected, even on her husband's days off, as it is Hell to juggle two jobs, a wife and a girlfriend at the same time.

So what else is a Carolina mother to do, with the smart little half black thing she is cursed with, when there are no screaming venom sprays to deliver, when there are no hot leather lashes to dispense. There is but the briefest and bizarre connection to gather, that is so gladly taken up by pretty young Tamela, the school pretty-girl, who all the white *and* little black boys grieve to get their ignorant little hands upon. What could they do beyond tremble in fear, at the sight of the undeveloped little breasts—

the puffy, half cooked areola muffins, where the growing nipple sits so raw, ready and exposed?

Little half white Tamela Lippincott. So Honor Society this and that already, so much the winner of every little spelling this or that, so much the winner of every little sixth grade academic this or that, until the "C" beatings are fewer and farther between. What else is there for a bored and lonely and desperate housewife to do, when she is not whipping her little girl's half white skin to blood? *The earthquake game is our secret,* the assy white mother would say, after the bathtub was run and filled, oh, so especially in the darkness of the winter days having come, when the daylight hours take their early and swift cold weather departure.

In the six o'clock darkness of this day among many, the tallish athletic little Amazon with the golden skin and little bubble butt, already clamps her little sucking lips upon her snow white mother's tit, leaving it there in a vacuum suck unreleased, while her mother's hand moves like a sword needle in a sewing machine on maximum between her own thighs, her face already twisted in the pre-agony, until her body explodes the energy inside her without ceasing, causing her to shake like an Armageddon earthquake, while she calls the name of God for mercy.

Tamela is witness to the violence of depravity unleashed, the striking of the underground well which hath erupted, and rumbled the earth and spewed a geyser in the aftermath of oblivion. This shaking of the earthquake, even when Tamela holds on tight to her grieving mother afterwards, feeling every rumbling aftershock still passing through. And this, not to the tune of false civility, as young Tamela knows that this secret is the lesser of every evil, and the worthy alternative to her mother's wrath unbridled and forlorn. And oh, how my sister and I must put on the false face of Hypocrisy, when we take the long drive east to Charlottesville, to make sure that Tamela Lippincott's husband and daughters, Tamela Wade's husband and daughters, are as gently exposed as possible, to where it is that their beloved wife and mother could have gone. This, to assuage the guilt, perhaps, that Tamela would not even have died on our country road, if my sister had not given her this fateful call. Oh, how we play naïve number one and innocent number one-A, when pretty blue eyed Jeff Wade says to Angela in my presence:

"I feel like its my fault she died. We'd had a little bit of an argument the day before she went to see you. Where I had judged her because of a little secret "earthquake game" she used to play with the girls.

"Earthquake game?"

"Yeah. Its has something to do with them shaking like their having a seizure or something, to see who can do it the best. I was taking the girls home from soccer practice, and I looked in the back seat at our youngest, and she was acting like she was hooked up to a live wire. I said 'what are you doing?' And she said while she was shaking, 'earthquake.' And her older sister smacked her on the thigh so hard, I said what was that for? And my youngest, the one who had been shaking, she sort of whispered— 'Mom didn't say we couldn't tell. And my oldest said 'shut up.' And so we all just sort of left it at that. But I was disturbed by it. I couldn't get it out of my head. And so that night, the night before she left to go to your house, I said 'Honey, did you teach Tina how to do something called an 'earthquake game?' And I will never forget the wave of fear that flashed over Tamela's face. It was a mixture of fear and shame. And without knowing the whole story, I sort of lit into her, judged her without really knowing what the Hell I was talking about. I said 'whatever it is you've taught them needs to stop. Because frankly, it looks like she was faking

an orgasm. And there is no way that an eleven year old girl would know how to do that on her own.' And Tamela got kind of mad. She said, 'what kind of dirty minded bullshit is this? Spoken like a true Presbyterian.' And I said 'its got nothing to do with that, it was just...inappropriate. And she said 'everything's inappropriate to you and your Amish mother and father...'

'Nobody's being Amish here, its just that when your eleven year old daughter looks like she faking the best orgasm I've ever seen says 'Mom didn't say we couldn't tell.... '

'Jeff, whatever, I can't listen to anymore of this crap, I've got a long day tomorrow, I've got to drive all the way to Woodland to see a colleague. You keep this dirty minded paranoia to yourself..."

And so, when *White And So* Pretty Jeff Wade asks Angela, *"Did your Mother ever teach you anything like that, or am I just naïve,"* Angela's mask of endtime hypocrisy is as intact as a white theater mask of ambiguity, when she says...

"If you knew my mother, you wouldn't have to ask."

So, we hug and pat Mr. Wade across his grieving back, leaving him to his shock and grief at his wife's passing, at his Vanessa Williams-faced, Kim Kardashian-assed wife's passing, to wonder for the rest of his unnatural life what the Hell an earthquake game is, and why it taught his little girl how to shake like she having an orgasm like it's the end of the world.

36

The rains over this eastern landscape fall with steady assurance, as every breath of wind blows in anger subdued, and end of the world power restrained. We stand alone, my sister and me, in the wake of every mourner of every class and color departed, content to be attacked by the force of every nearby drop of rain, and every broken gust of wind. The cemetery landscape is a mist of gray past the field of gravestones and markers, over the plush, green forest grove, and far off into the distance, where streaks of lightning flash from the bottom of the clouds with controlled fury. Even so, we stand un-idly in the midst of this deadly storm in our hooded black raincoats, our umbrellas down at my sister's behest, now unafraid to stand among the dancing shears of white and blue lightning.

We are bound to pay our respects to the dishonored dead. To the first victim we are cursed to know, the first victim of the curse that I am, and the dark energy I have brought screaming into this world. This strange and powerful storm flashes in bitterness overhead, as if to ask angrily why we mourn this woman's passing, to place the words in my spirit *"let the dead bury the dead,"* causing me to flinch against my sister, who stands fast before Tamela's grave as though in waiting, to see what possible end time message there is to be given, in the midst of this storm of eschatology.

In the grips of this energy that flows, I am briefly lifted up and transported back to places unknown, to sights and sounds unwanted, by the upper middle class dwelling of the Wade family, in a pocket of space somewhere in their brief yesterday. I see two beautiful girls of Latin appearance, eleven and twelve years old respectively, so happily nude in the presence of their beautiful golden skinned mother, so full breasted in broad hipped nudity in this locked bathroom, where the father is away on innocent business. I see the woman of great learning, this woman of Princeton, by way of this state's largest university—I see this exquisite, middle aged beauty in the shapeliness of fertility, so gleefully playing her game of eschatology with her two daughters, her game that foreshadows the Battle of Armageddon.

I see the eleven year old little daughter, naked while the shower fills the grand bathroom with mist, with her naked mother's breasts in both hands, vacuum sucking both breasts back and forth in rapid succession, sucking, pulling in playful popping sound, as the middle aged mother shakes her head no in growling, bellowing disbelief that such heightened sensation is possible in the human body, her spirit briefly flashing to her

siren of hopelessness, where the daughters continue their rubbing and sucking rhythms, until the mother's wailing siren transforms into a noisy weeping, followed by a deep, bellowing madness of the voice, trembled in full bodied spasms from the top of her head to the soles of her feet. She rests in the torture of this madness, content to suffer the Quaking of Nod, grunting and shaking in agony, as her daughters continue their unmerciful rhythms unbeknownst and undeterred.

Undisturbed by the driving rhythm of the storm, my sister stands behind me tall and strong, looking over my shoulder at the freshly dug grave of the woman we barely knew, undaunted by the flashes of lightning from the clouds, and the rumbling voice of doom from one end of creation to the other.

37

The essence of Cleopatra lurks around us in the shadows, in our nighttime bed of grief and mourning. Whatever pretenses, whatever false notions Angela may have had for what we are seem to have been swept up into the winds of this storm, and carried away on a current of nighttime fury. For some strange reason, Angela had found on old outfit reminiscent of a Catholic school girl, and come downstairs to where I was watching TV. Complete with the vest, short skirt, knee high black socks and loose ponytail. I was amazed by the frightening, bizarre beauty of what I saw, when she sat down on the big, plush sofa beside me and crossed her leg with a wry smile barely detectable.

It is a set of secret clothing that decorates the back of her closet, bought for her by the cello teacher, which she had worn many times in private in years past. The look of epic, feined humility on her face is enthralling, made complete by words she speaks in Cantonese that strikes me like lightning in the storm. But after all, why wouldn't a Chinese woman with an undergraduate Ivy League degree in physics, who was taught the cello by a world renown cello teacher—why wouldn't she be hiding such an end of the world shock for my pathetic soul? When she had opened her mouth in Cantonese for *"please forgive me for disturbing you mistress Caley,"* I had actually laughed a high pitch sound that shocked me into putting my hand over my own mouth.

She then has mercy on me and breaks the spell, talking to me in English again about how silly she knows she looks, and about how *"some clichés are classic, aren't they"* she says, of which my soul responds that truth and beauty are God's weapons against hypocrisy. This living fantasy, this disturbing life sized China doll moves closer to me on the plush, gray sofa and says in my ear something in Cantonese, which she repeats in English *"please forgive me for needing to be punished. Will you come to the bathroom with me?"*

Without looking at me at all, this Chinese beauty stands up tall and lovely, and walks away quickly towards the stairs, disappearing from my awestruck gaze up the stairs into the hall. The nerves that seem to accompany every session of ours have reappeared in full, delaying my response, until I have to force myself to get up, and push myself though the fear. I swim in the wake of this ghostly memory, following it up the stairs, turning down the hallway to the master bath, where she stands at the mirror with her hands clasped in front of her, looking like a total stranger to me, as if she walked through a doorway from another place, and wound up in our bathroom in front of the mirror.

"Please close the door," she says, her American voice slipping away totally by accident, I think. *"I have not been good enough,"* she says. *"I have not done my job."* I watch this grown woman, my savior woman, the difference between my luxury and my destitution, take her vest off and place it neatly on the counter nearby the wooden ruler, and begin to unbutton the white blouse with some strange, academic looking shield on the breast pocket, pushed out so incredibly far by what lies beneath. The contrast between this typical schoolgirl innocence, and the cleavage that rises as the buttons continue to fall is exhilarating on every level to me, as I watch her look down with such fearful demurity, without any knowing smile to break the tension.

White shirt still tucked in, she reaches into her bra and pulls out two of the biggest breasts in all of God's creation, clearly at least three or four times larger than the average so called busty woman could hope for, a C-4 explosion for the senses, framed by the white blouse opened around them. The twinge I suddenly feel in my groin is certainly born from the Curlingale blood passed down, which causes my heart to beat faster, and my breathing to suddenly go slow and deep. She hands me the ruler, which I take in quiet disbelief, as if there is no way she expects me to actually hit her with this.

"Because I have been so unworthy," she says, *"you have to punish me until I cry. My breasts are too big, Caley San. They need to be punished too hard until I learn to obey."*

What can I do, but swallow my own fear and comply? As she turns to the mirror, I take my place beside her, the ruler in my right hand, unable to keep from smiling to a near giggle, until I notice the solemn look in her expression. I take the ruler and begin to pitifully tap the top of her breasts away from the nipple, as if I don't understand fully what this is, and what pains there are that need to be dispensed.

"Punish my nipples," she says. *"Punish me until I need to cry."*

And so this, I do. Tapping the ruler against her nipples like I mean it, shocked by her sudden, new reaction, which is a full on squinting of the eyes, and a teeth clenching grimace of the mouth. But what is this sleeping dragon you have awakened in me, my poor sister? The painful reaction sends a chill from my heart straight to my groin, which gives me an instinct I've never had. A new instinct, fed by the natural human instinct for cruelty.

I am suddenly in need to see her suffer from what this little ruler can do to these Olympian bosoms. And so, I begin to play the Rhythm of the Nuns on her nipple, until she is suddenly regretful that she gave this machine gun to a novice, who doesn't know when to let up off the trigger. She begins to yelp very loudly in the echoing space, but trained not to move beyond the bare minimum, to stand still and let the pain out through her voice. Something prompts me to switch to the other nipple, which brings a lesser cry of something akin to relief.

This, I continue. Playing this rhythm from one great breast to the other, even across the ivory white skin to stripe it so deeply red, until the melancholy in her expression grows to a place of grief, and the pain in her eyes grows to a place of sorrow. As if she didn't really believe it until it began, her tolerance for the pain crumbles and falls away, and I am thrilled beyond measure, to watch this grown woman break down and begin to weep from the pain.

I hit her once more with a flurry of blows, brought to my senses by this last scream and shaking of her head *'no,'* where it seems that the pain has crossed over into something she cannot endure.

"I still have to learn," she says, sniffing, wiping her eyes. *"I need to learn not to be a whore in my mind."*

Her face red and anguished, fully wet with tears, she takes my hand and places it under her skirt, pressing it to the soft, swollen warmth of the hidden cloth underneath.

"Rub me under my skirt," she says, *"until I can learn my place. Until I can obey."*

She puts her hands behind her back, as I begin to stroke the soft linen cloth underneath, the underwear cloth, where I can feel her swollen to a great proportion, and the heat of blue and black fire burning within. Over the cloth, I continue this rubbing, watching the anguish in her expression transform to another kind, this, the frustration of waiting, to receive the rewards of a promise made. I explore this rubbing under her skirt, until I find the place at the center of longing, where I see her eyes close, and hear the exclamation point made in her breath.

I find this new motion, to place her on the road to devastation, the full truth of punishments made and given. She can only look at me pitifully, in prayer that I keep her on this road to ruin, to break the tension that has built up in her mind, body and spirit...

And as if obeying an inner voice, I reach down and gently pull her nipple into my mouth, amazed at the long, *whoo*-ing sound that suddenly flows from her, followed by the violent breaking of the tension in her body, causing me to have to struggle to hold her steady.

Jonathan Lovejoy

Clash of the Lady Titans

38

*T*hunder rolls over our nighttime resolve, where my sore breasted benefactor sleeps soundly after her latest trauma, with me tucked in safely in front of her, her arm wrapped tightly around my waist. Oddly enough, though I was the one who was doing all the punishing, why do I feel so devastated inside? And I know that she is lost in one of the best sleeps she has had in a long time, as if every nerve in her body has been calmed to tranquility.

Where do our darkest motivations hearken from? What keeps the psychiatrists in business year in and year out, where there are hardly enough of them available to keep up with demand? Especially since the eve of the Second Coming has begun to unfurl, where the entire population can feel the rising tide of eschatology. There is a pervasive fear that is spreading, where people are losing their way, with moral compasses spiraling out of control, so that people have no discernible direction in which to travel. We are all adrift as autumn leaves in a cold, November wind.

These two have gathered in a place of warmth and refuge, the beautiful Asian woman and me, taking time away from our journey upon the four winds, to begin to accept our Fate as two unfulfilled promises in life, struck down by the tragedy of what is meant to be. How could I have known that I was going to disappear like a ghost in the wind, and materialize 20 years down the timeline, to see and feel the world around me as part of a waking dream, with only this strange, exotic woman beside me to keep it all from feeling like a waking nightmare instead?

And how could this lonely woman have known, that despite her flight through the academic world, despite her training on the cello with the world famous cello teacher, despite her slide through Yale University, and then the fun PhD trip through the solar system by way of the University of Virginia—how could Angela have known that despite these assets, she would continue to be a victim of her mother's sickness, to have become a slave to it herself, so that her mind and body will both begin to slip out of equilibrium without this perversion? How was Angela Tao to know that twenty years after her sister's lost trip to Virginia Beach, that she would get a call from her father, and walk into the house to see an end of the world sign in blonde, blue eyed truth appear? Angela Tao could not have known that on the afternoon she received her PhD in Physics and Astronomy, her mother would remind her that she was not graduating *away* from her control, but was graduating deeper *into* it.

I can see the vitriol in her eyes, dear sister. I can feel the bitterness in her soul, when you receive your doctorate degree from the University, but hidden behind the mask of cultured civility, the mask of Rich Woman Hypocrisy—where the truth is hidden with such depth and skill as to be undetectable by all. Such a wildly prestigious Mother Daughter team you are, Dear Angela, the forty something year old wife of a lucky, rich lawyer named Littledove, adopted mother of the most beautiful Asian woman any of them have ever seen. They watch Doctor Tao start this happy journey to absolutely nowhere, wished farewell in tears and hugs and kisses from the beautiful mother, white beauty queen, suburban charity queen. Why do so many of them want a picture with that Asian woman and her white mother? They're not famous. Who is it that they think they are?

The argument starts as soon as the car door shuts.

"I already let you change your goddamned last name and that's as far as its gonna go."

"Mom, I think I've earned the right to teach wherever I want. I'm going to Florida and that's it."

"Why would you want to go all the way to Florida when they offered you a teaching job right here?"

"Do you know how lame it is to teach at the same school where you got your PhD?"

"What?"

"You heard me. You're just announcing to the world how pathetic and scared you were to leave the nest."

"I don't understand how a degree from Yale and the University of Virginia can be pathetic no matter where you teach."

"That's because you're not a college professor, Mom, whose basically a glorified failed scientist. You think I want to spend the next 10 years trying not to make eye contact with everybody knowing I couldn't get on as an astronomer anywhere? Its like they all saw right through me. 'You've got the name, the face, the grades, but we're looking for scientists honey, not scholars. Good luck in your teaching career.' One of the pricks even had the nerve to ask me out on a date while he was not taking my application seriously. Well if I'm gonna teach then I'm getting as far away from this crummy school as I can get."

"You're only saying the school is crummy because you went there. I guarantee there is a busload of rejects who would sell their souls for a doctorate from there, honey. Believe me."

There is no sweetness in this honey, is there my Sweet? My dearest Angela, my tragedy in eastern beauty? There is the hornet's sting nearby this honeycombe, where the pet name 'honey' is given in bitterness, and with the lightning strike of warning.

"So you think I'm just going to let you leave here and go to wherever the Hell you want?"

"It's my life, Mom. Isn't it? Why in God's name didn't I just stick with the cello?"

And it is here I see, my dearest Angela, the door into your life opened again. Words, and the power of the tongue. I do not see the wave, but from where I am, I feel it flow through our mother, to raise the agony of her temper again, but which she takes a deep breath in an effort to fight, so that the two of you can make it home without incident. Are you aware, Angela, as you drive these darkened, upper class suburban streets of this town? As the two of you turn the corner onto the black asphalt driveway, in the earthen shadows of the evening day? Are you aware, dear Angela, of the source of pain, the pain of rage, the rage that begins the cycle of fear? Has it been too long, Angela, since Mother has reminded you of who she is?

Mother escorts your twenty six year old self this time, down the concrete walkway up to the front door, where Mother Daughter time in the cooking kitchen awaits, so that you can put seven pounds back onto your breasts and hips where they belong. So that you and she can finalize your plans, your steps, your path chosen in this life. What can she do, dear Angela, but shut up and cut the green peppers, while you cut the onions and the pieces of tender beef? This is the day, Dr. Tao, that Mother learns who it is you think you are, is it not?

Step confidently into your fine house, dear sister. Have the smiling hope knocked off your face in the haze of a slow motion dream...

Feel the tension of choking at your throat. Feel the scratching of nails climbing your thighs underneath your long skirt pulled up. What lovely black boots are these, pretty Asian schoolgirl? What lovely long, charcoal gray fabric is this, pulled up from the boots?

Yelp this warning through the choking, my dear, when the pinch on your inner thigh clamps down in warning. Try and suppress the shock and the scream in your throat, when the pinching moves to the front of your underwear cloth. As to the pain and fear it flows, you cannot tell. Jerk your body in hopelessness to escape. Marvel the near masculine strength she possesses, channeled through the vengeance of the feminine. Do you wish to fight her, Angela? You cannot. As she presses her face to yours. Not in a kiss but in a push.

What words do you hear her breathe forth to thee? She doesn't know who the *"fuck"* this Mom person is you've been talking too, she says, but for the rest of your *"fucking"* life you will call her *"Mother."* Is the agony pinched between your legs at this moment quite enough, Dear Angela? It is not. For the defiance in your scream. The lack of humility. The insolence. You *"fucking cunt,"* dear Angela. Another pinch is there. To remind you as you scream again, that to be born is to be cursed.

And to live is to suffer.

39

$\mathscr{A}$s it is written, there is often so much to fear, from a fateful knocking at the door. The aftermath of the latest pair of eyes lit up in this storm is a strong tapping at the front door, and a mad scramble by my sister to make herself presentable. A quick draping of burgundy cloth over her favorite black sports bra and long, loose ponytail untied accomplishes this, while our pitiful, wet visitor waits for her surprised hostesses to come to the door.

Angela opens the door into the voice of the storm, to hear the warning in the rain, and to invite the Greek-Italian beauty into our country home. Smiles, hugs and kisses all around, brought forth by the spirit of *fungalooga,* and the inability to expose the dreariness of what churns beneath cultured civility.

Adelia Evanopoulos is all of six feet in her heels. A model of Amazonian strength and beauty, with a full length dress of navy cloth hopelessly pushed out at the top, in grieving to hide the macromastic truth of what lies beneath. A strong armed, man-handed woman of substance and extraordinary, exotic appeal, looking as though she could caress one's soul into bliss, or choke it into blue faced oblivion. Her black hair is tightly pinned, to reveal a face with depth and unearthly sensuality, with a bright smile and deep, hypnotic eyes, a stare from which could surely bring a man or careless woman to ruin. One of two goddesses, who hug and laugh in front of me like long, lost companions who had been away, but somehow found a way to come back together again.

"And who is this living doll," she says, staring at me in Old World seriousness, unsettling once and for all what few nerves I have left. Scaring the crap out of me.

"Adelia, this is my sister Caley." Angela says it with such pathetic, prepackaged phoniness that it nearly makes her sick, hearing the fake-assed smile in her own voice, *'anelia...niss is my nister naley...'* is the whiny, mocking voice in her head that runs a chill up her spine.

"Your *sister?*" Adelia says, refusing to descend to complete, whiny phoniness, but having mercy on us and not asking the obvious question. "Your sister is beautiful," she says, taking me by both sides of the face and kissing me full on the lips, moaning deeply enough to send a tingle to my groin. She smacks away this kiss with passion, leaving the imprint of soft lips, lipstick and chocolate in my soul forever.

"Your eyes," she says, shaking her head *no,* "are as blue as the ocean. Could you do me big favor, Sweetie? Could you lend me your sister for a while? We've got something strange and private to discuss. Please forgive me for being rude, Sweet Girl."

I happily take this cue, bounding my blonde, bubble headedness upstairs, so glad to get as far away from this literary pair as possible, this reunion of the goddesses, this clash of the lady titans, this annihilation born when worlds collide. The Asian beauty looks up so slowly from the floor where she was staring. Struggling by sheer will power, until she makes eye contact with the beautiful woman from her dreams, from the landscape of her most distant memory. Their eyes meet upon a rumbling from the clouds, the storm's acknowledgment of a reunion six years in the making. As if obeying a voice from the gloom and the gray, the Asian girl steps firmly to the beautiful older woman, laying her head on her shoulder as they hold one another, in an embrace so ripe with fear.

"*I*t was my mother. She made me stop."

"I pushed too hard," Adelia says. "I wanted us to tour Europe for God's sake. Have you ever head of anything so ridiculous?"

"It *was* ridiculous," Angela whispers, looking at the mature beauty. The contrast in their ages is apparent, with Adelia comfortable on the voluptuous side of fifty, looking old enough to be the Asian beauty's mother in spirit. Theirs is a dynamic of power. An attraction born of forces irresistible, and beyond their comprehension. The younger woman reaches up to her former mistress's lips, planting a full kiss upon them, causing the older woman to recoil from the power coursing through.

"But what about your sister?"

"She won't see us."

"But I don't..."

The older woman's words are interrupted by her former lover's lips, causing her to breathe through her body's brief tremble. She lets her embrace become that of desperation unfurled, hugging the shorter, younger Asian woman with strength and power, nearly lifting her off her feet as she gives in to the energy around them. In the living room, nearby the stairs in full view, the women kiss a fervent kiss, to engage their bodies in the agony of renewal, and their spirits in the trauma of a blissful reunion. When the kiss is done, as the breaths of life are taken, Adelia glimpses toward the stairs, in fear of what pair of blue eyes might be lurking in secret.

"I didn't come here for this," she says pitifully. "I swear it to *God* I didn't."

"I know," Angela says, sniffing away the tears. She takes Adelia by the hand, to the chorus of voices that cascade from the clouds of doom, leading her over to the sofa. She looks into the somber eyes of her mistress resurrected, fascinated by the Amazonian strength reduced to weakness, and the fortress of her resolve now devastated to ruin.

"When you left," Adelia says, "I thought I was going to *die.*" Her voice rises up from a whisper on the last syllable, so deep with the sorrow of the ages, in Estros burdened by the touch of Testros' hand.

"I almost died too, Adelia. But you don't know the power my mother has over me. The power she has over my life."

"I understand. Believe me I do. I had a mother once too, you know. She's gone now, but she was very demanding. And I've been Hell with my own daughters, I'll admit. So, I really do understand."

"Why exactly did you come here?"

Adelia composes herself. Requisite sniffing and face wiping done. The shapely, mature brunette stands up strong and tall again, and wanders in regal repose to the huge bay window.

"This storm is spreading," she says. "Its across three states now."

"It's an end of the world storm," Angela says. "I don't think there's been anything quite like it. In some ways, its seems worse than a hurricane. The tornado sightings increase every day. The lightning's so bad its smart not to go outside at all if you don't have to."

"I wouldn't have come if it wasn't important. I think…this storm is a reflection of how the world feels. The growing bitterness. The anger. The perversion."

She turns to look in the eyes of her former lover.

Fearlessly.

"Maybe I'm a part of this storm," she says. "Maybe I'm part of what's feeding it. Giving it life."

"Why? Because of us?"

"I was a married woman, with daughters of my own. You trusted me. I had no right."

"You had every right," Angela says, "to reach out to me in love. I could have refused. But I didn't."

"I reached out to you in *lust*, Angela. What kind of a woman does that make me? What kind of a monster?"

"It makes you a woman of passion. Of conviction. You have a power that most other people could only dream of. Adelia, you have a successful family. You're a world famous musician. And you're one of the world's most beautiful women. And if you were a monster, you couldn't have loved me."

"I'll admit," Adelia says, "I thought about you every day. I even neglected my own daughters because of you. After you left, I went cold to them. And my husband. I focused on my instrument again. And that's really why I'm here. Do you still play?"

"Sometimes, but just as a hobby."

Adelia looks away from the window briefly, to where the cello rests silently on the stand.

"The last time heard you play Bach's prelude, I remember that I expected to hear my voice coming from your instrument. The way that I taught you to play it. With precision. But what I heard... was *your* voice. I wanted, at first, to walk over to you and clobber your hand with my stick. But I listened. And what I heard, maybe for the first time in the... I don't know... the hundred times I've heard it... I heard the voice of God himself. And it was terrifying in its beauty. Its purity. It wasn't just another series of those nasal notes, stroking and whining again. It was a message being *spoken* to me. A message of rage restrained by beauty. A voice of sorrow repressed by joy. It was a warning about the coming end of the world, Angela. A warning that God himself spoke to me when you played. And now, I can barely stand to hear anyone else play it. They're just making a clumsy mess of it. Too fast. Too slow. Too stiff. To relaxed. They never know how long to hold that last note. Inevitably, it's a disaster. Yours was the only perfect playing of that piece I've ever heard. Better than any concert. Any recording...

And that's why I'm here, Angela. I was approached by a record company. One of the biggest classical labels in the world, to record the cello suites. Big money offer and everything. Every classical musician's dream. Her exact words to me were, *'We need to fight for our music before it dies.'* And to tell you the truth, she's right. All the new young artists coming up have all got some ridiculous angle—like this pissy little *twit,* God forgive me, this little *thing* their marketing on our instrument now, every time I see her face—every time I hear about her goddamned Christmas album it makes me sick to my stomach. Nobody wants to play classical music anymore. *'We need some beauty on our instrument that still wants to play Mozart.'* When she said that, your face and your name popped in my head. *'I know a cellist,'* I said. *'She's Asian. Gifted. And impossibly beautiful. She was my private student for seven years,'* I said. *'Her name is Angela Tao...'*

"The look on her face let me know, Angela. I had to come here. I had to ask. I had to brave this storm, for a girl that has a calling. Even though I know, that even you, with your gifted playing, could never reproduce that sound I heard that day."

Without a word, Angela is unable to stay in place, rising up immediately, strolling over to the cello boldly, to the look of admiration and quiet warning in her teacher's eyes.

"No," she says. Holding up her hand. "I want to remember it just the way I heard it that day."

"I need to play it for you, Delia."

"You already have, Honey. A thousand times."

Adelia Evanopoulos rides the wind. The Winds of Eschatology. The rain and winds on the streets of this town, away from the Road to Woodland. To the proud, pristine property of privilege. Where her pills and glass of wine are her secret pride and joy.

Adelia rides the wind and the miles. Cast out into the storm by another. Tossed out into this end of the world deluge by hopeless longing. By a failed resurrection of the dead. Told by the Asian beauty, *'you record the music, Delia. Its not for me.'* Being told 'no' when every cell in your body once coalesced to one mind, to feed you a false prophecy of 'yes.' The two of you together in recording studios. In concert. Live around the world. You as a guest of hers on record and on stage in duets for the cello. To resurrect the instrument in beauty. To speak God's message to a dying world. His warning messages in beauty and song.

Adelia Evanopoulos rides the wind. The winds of all hope having come and gone. Her last chance at a reprieve. Her last chance at Redemption. A last barrier raised. A buffer between her and the grave. A cushion to protect her in the fall. A last refuge in this storm of eschatology.

She hears the cello sing its song of sorrow. One last message to a soul adrift in the storm. Rising high, falling swiftly on the tide of notes played. Flowing along smoothly toward its inevitable conclusion. Being held in such rapture at the end of time, to the moment when the last note sets to unfurl, not believing it to be possible until it happens. When the last note of the prelude phases her into a ghostly hue, to pull her along in phantasm, to phase her in a continuous stream of hope and faith for a reprieve—she is removed from this evil space and dimension, and carried by this conduit cello string, to the shores of Paradise and eternity.

Adelia Evanopoulos rides the wind. The Winds of Eschatology. To the house of pride and privilege.

Where awaits the pills and a glass of wine.

Jonathan Lovejoy

In League of

Passion

y mother's screams burn the theater of her mind, as she enters me from behind without mercy. I am no longer an anal virgin, as the pain of my sister's member strapped on fills the back of me with a fervent heat, and a burden of blue and black fire. The colors of her black leather harness and royal blue member notwithstanding, I decorate the walls of her bedroom with the vibrations of my screams, energy for the ears and the soul, rather than the eyes and the mind. What pain this is, is surely channeled from her inner self into me as a victim, pain born from two ravens having paid us a visit a few days after her cello teacher left. The two daughters of Adelia Evanopoulos, two exquisitely exotic, younger versions of herself, with hair as black a raven's feathers, with piercing eyes to match, and a power in their presence that must surely enrapture

their audience when they are on the cello and the piano. The oldest being he lesser of the two beauties, the one who had failed to learn her mother's instrument, who plays the piano in a cloud of defeat and regret, as compensation for having been a failure in her mother's eyes, who was literally beaten by her mother when she could not learn to play the instrument without error. The piano was her natural progression, the place where she could hide in mediocrity, which is profound excellence for the trained and untrained ear. Hers was the voice of repressed bitterness, though not toward Angela and me. It was the repressed rage of a daughter who had become emotionally neglected over the years—who was the object of her mother's wrath and ridicule rather than kindness and compassion. And besides all this, now there was the delivery of this end of the world tragedy of news to us, that her mother had been found dead in her bed one afternoon, a victim of what two different kinds of bottles may hold—one of pills, and the other of a glass of wine. When the older raven spoke this tragedy to us, the younger and more beautiful raven bowed her sweet head and sobbed once from lack of control, where a genuine tear decorated the skin of a face so fair.

In the heart of this memory, all that Angela can do is put her hand over her mouth and stare at the two of them as if the are pure-tee ghosts, two phantoms raised up from a stormy cemetery somewhere, charged with finding and infusing her life with unearthly fear and dread. The look of shock and devastation on Angela's face had served to assuage the growing bitterness inside this older daughter, I think, which made the Adina Raven more receptive to carrying out her mother's death wish from her will. And even this, only from pressure from her mother's husband, from her father, who had to force her to go to Angela as her mother had stated in the will, to deliver her the thing in life that she had loved the most.

In the rains of this grieving memory, Angela and I wait patiently and bewilderedly, as the Adina and the Athena raven go back out into the storm that sent them to us in the first place, and retrieve the heavy instrument from their SUV. To them, it is a heavy and cumbersome thing, a grim reminder of what they have lost, and by what horrific manner they have lost it. Of what purpose could their mother's cello really serve them, accept as a painful echo of where it is that their beloved mother could have gone?

And this, along with a briefcase sized, locked wooden box, *"only to be opened by Angela Tao upon my death,"* the new will had said. When the two dark ravens had flown back to the netherworld from whence they had come, back to the netherworld from which they came, Angela and me had unlocked and opened the shiny, darkwood treasure chest, intrigued if not quite disappointed, to see a lovely, simple little ivory card, with the words inside in red ink—*"with love, my dearest Angela,"* the name *Adelia* signed in league of passion. Inside this ivory card is a check from a record label (whose name hearkens the misty regions of Great Britain's capital city), a check made out to Adelia, a high six figure amount that would have devastated any younger, poorer artist to be sure with joy and laughter. But the truest, and perhaps most fascinating of treasures lays underneath this card and check, a CD with an impossibly alluring, mature woman on the cover, bearing resemblance to some unknown opera diva of otherworldly beauty, a picture bearing the music of her name, and that of the name Bach, and the treasures of his six Cello Suites newly recorded in full, to be released posthumously, played by the Greek-Italian beauty seen on the cover.

I wonder if this is the fullness of the agony I feel, pushing into my rectum from behind—pressed heavy upon my back in our position on all fours, squeezed and pulled heavy on both my sore tits by just one of her hands, squeezing and pulling without mercy from one to the other. I wonder, what of the infinity of travesties flows through her mind at this moment, as she takes the pain of living out on me, projecting it onto my flesh in brief, strong pinches, spanks and chokings, restrained out of pure love and respect, but registered as a warning to the future of my place along the timeline. I wonder if it is the sound of our mother's screams that beckon her now, from when she was ordered to do this to our own mother in the wealthy suburban estate, where Mother's healthy buttocks had been spanked raw beforehand, and the strapped on member pushed in anally from behind.

Is it the bizarre, animalistic yelling, the cry of pain and anger from our mother, that tenses and torments Angela's flesh to its plateau while she presses against me? As she twists and pulls my nipples downward enough to make me have to cry out in pain, is it *my* screaming, or the screams of Ja'net Littledove, that cause Angela's hips to lurch forward on their own, and her voice to rise the heights of an end of the world siren in wailing, weeping, and gnashing of teeth?

The storm over Virginia has grown in size and strength, reaching out to West Virginia and the Carolinas, feeding upon the warm, summer waters off the coasts of Virginia Beach and Cape Hatteras, until the overall pattern of these clouds grows dangerously circular, with powerful gusts of wind that rival that of a category we-know-not-what, with one meteorologist speaking the word itself saying: *"Folks, if I didn't know any better I would say that this thing was a hurricane…"* but defying all logic of one, having been born from a single thunderstorm over Roanoke

County. The storm grew in size until it reached all the way to the Atlantic, and has been growing in power ever since.

And I have noticed that what behind closed doors power I am now a prisoner of has grown in proportion with the winds and the rains outside, until I have to remind myself that unlike the floodwaters that have washed bridges and roads away around the state, the floodwaters of Angela's contempt are as brief thundershowers alone, meant to rain down upon me only a quick flash flood of terror. Despite the lengthy and painful spankings, breast bitings, belt whippings, canings, smotherings, chokings, hair pullings and the like, I know that her concern for me otherwise has not changed, as these brief tortures are sometimes delivered in laughter and pain.

But I move forward bravely, determined to help her deal with the accumulation of strangeness her life has heaped upon her, the latest being the second victim of this end of the world storm we know, and the presence of a cello she left behind. It has taken its place nearby her own instrument for the time being, so that the spirits may now engage their ghostly duets somewhere beyond our hearing.

What I love the most is when my sister rapes me. When she grabs me by the hair with both hands until I see lightning, with the extension of her inner self already strapped on, bending my head down with both hands to *"choke on her cock"* as she says, to watch me choke, gag and spit helplessly upon it, until I am looking up at her with tears flowing down my face of their own volition, born from the trauma of choking I suppose, rather than pain or sorrow. These two are reserved for the things I don't like so much, especially the lengthy and severe canings, which reduce me to weeping on a grand scale, which I know races her heart to light speed. *"Shut your mouth,"* she'll say, her accent waxing Asian so mysteriously.

"Little blonde bitch cry too much." But I know it is this crying that she loves to hear, as she has become more ruthless and merciless in what she does, until I am so often amazed by the severity of the welts, cuts and bruises I see in the mirror, especially across my buttocks and the backs of my thighs.

"You've got Mom's hips already," she says, which is a curse as far as I'm concerned, giving me sort of a big, wide bubble butt that is somewhat terrifying to consider; if my ass is that big now, what's gonna happen when I'm 40? And she'll say, *"Mom's ass, Future Girl."* Which is truly every teenage girl's worst nightmare. I guess I'm Iggy Azalea assed after all, and probably should be proud of it but I'm not. Why do other girl's big, shapely butts look so good on them and so bad on ourselves? A mystery, I think, as unsolvable as the one that transported me to this strange place I'm in.

What strange place it is, indeed, where you must be beaten and raped by your sister! The many intense face slappings and severe hair pullings, sometimes with her twisting both my nipples at once while I stand in the middle of the bedroom floor with my hands behind my back, her telling me to *"shut [my] spoiled little mouth,"* and to *"cry when you have something better to cry for."* Here, her mood will often change to the severe, and I will get slapped so much harder than usual, which hurts so much deeper than my skin. This will shut me up in voice, but not in weeping, as the tears will start to flow this time from pain and sorrow. *"Get your little fat ass over to that bed, future girl,"* she'll say, so very sharply sometimes, where the seed of her lifetime of bitterness is nurtured and grown.

In the blast of endtime thunder I hear, my face burns from the blast of my sister's rape slap to my face, which sends me to the bed in tears, where I feel a massive hair pull, pulling my head up, with her hand tightly around my throat, with her looking me in the eye with a new energy, where something in her has crossed over, to where the fear I feel is not the thrill of exhilaration but the fear of bodily harm. It has risen to a higher place than the staged little assaults I have grown to enjoy, but carries with it the dark energy of something sinister, something deeper into this forest of the forbidden.

By my throat, Angela slams me to the bed in the lady dragon fire, then slams herself on top of me, with her hand at my throat tight enough to make me cough. I am suddenly plunged into a chasm, an outer darkness of dread and sorrow, feeling the cold wind of betrayal, and the icy breath of it in my lungs. I am suddenly more afraid during this than I've ever been, wondering where this bitterness, this anger is coming from, and whether I've done something to deserve it.

But all pretense of her intensions are suddenly pushed away, when she pushes the first inch times eight into the front of me, where I know to open my legs back far and wide, while she slides herself all the way up into me un-gently, to where it hurts this time, causing me to cry out in pain. This only serves her purpose though, I know, causing her an involuntary shudder while she pins my arms far back underneath me, holding them there with one hand and covering my mouth with the other. And she begins her requisite rabbit rhythm, pounding into me very hard and fast, until she takes her hand from my mouth and wraps her arms around me, slamming herself into me lightning quick, a rhythm which gets to me in a place beyond pain and fear, until my high pitched squeaking grows louder and longer into a squeal, which explodes into many quick, high pitched screams of terrifying pleasure shooting through my body.

And in the midst of my hopeless hollering, somewhere near my ear, I hear the deep, desperate bellowing of an animal, an animal that is a woman, banging down on top of me with a strength and speed that I know she couldn't stop if she tried.

The Echo Chamber of Holies

The rains fall with steady assurance, attacking our journey and arrival to this prestige funeral gathering. This part of the world has been called and chosen as one of many, to remind Creation of the rainbow promise, and the possibilities of 40 days and 40 nights from ancient history. With my sister behind the wheel of my mother's black SUV, we were forced to take an alternate road out of town, as the east end road to Woodland Falls was partially covered by an angry Woodland stream, overflowed to pure fascination, rushing from one side of the wooded highway to the next. The small bridge had been underneath just enough water to be impassable, with the water pouring through and over the little country bridge railings, to warn the approaching cars of any impending fool's errand. I remember wondering if any fish had chosen this path over the railing, as my sister had turned the SUV around in nervous awe. And though I never said it, these strange waters seemed to emanate from some unknown source, as if poured into our world from another dimension, perhaps even the one that I am cursed to have seen on my nighttime trip, taken no more than just six weeks ago. Still, I move through space like a fresh wound unhealed, still raw to the touch, my whole existence a source of great pain, fear and trepidation.

From the back seat of our SUV journey, I can barely make out the dark shapes drifting to and fro in the rain, carried to this devastation in their own laps of luxury, each having arrived on the current of their own Wealthen Stream. We disembark our rolling chariot in the grieving wind and mist, where it seems that every car and half car, truck and half truck in the world is the color of storm and night. We join the gathering of old money, art world phantoms and occasional luminaries, all gathered under a heady, high-minded spirit far exceeding that of the Virginia University woman's burial, to where it seems that somewhere in the crowd might be someone of unearthly importance who might appear.

Apparently, Adelia Evanopoulos stretched a network of travelers far and wide, many of who hearken on energy that rises from the East, appearing in the world in like manner as my sister. And as we walk up the high stairs to the great stone cathedral, my sister spies the brightest star at this end of the world farewell, a world reknowned cellist whose ability *so, so far* exceeds the heights of the ordinary and the mundane. Moreso than Mother and me, my sister can hardly take another breath without her hand at her chest and her mouth open in rapt amazement.

Nearby where we sit in the crowded church cathedral, in the presence of angels captured in the tall stained glass windows, we can see the two black crows of our recent memory, the two beautiful daughters of the lady cellist, all set to lead the congregation in the worship of Beauty's posthumous pride of life.

"And it shall come to pass in the last days, saith God, I will pour out of my spirit upon all flesh: and your sons and your daughters shall prophesy, and your young men shall see visions, and your old men shall dream dreams…

And on my servants and on my hand maidens I will pour out in those days of my spirit; and they shall prophesy.

And I will show wonders in Heaven above, and signs in the earth beneath; blood and fire, and vapour of smoke:

The sun shall be turned to darkness, and the moon into blood, before that great and notable day of the Lord come:

And it shall come to pass, that whosoever shall call on the name of the Lord shall be saved…

"Its very hard to look around us nowadays without being reminded of what theologians call the eschatological calendar, the flow of events leading to the so called end of days. I had the privilege of speaking to this lovely woman whom we honor today. I had the privilege of hearing her prophesy on her instrument of choice. And when I spoke to her the last time, she was burdened by the idea that the world was on the edge of something powerful, something beyond the dramatic, something that has not been since the dawn of time.

"And I was among those lucky enough to be in the presence of this unassuming woman, who was beautiful enough to get as much attention as any woman would ever have needed, but who shunned the limelight for as long as she could in the music world, until finally she got the calling, to be the cello's voice of beauty to an endtime generation. To share with the world what prophecies she may have received from the mind of our Lord and Savior, speaking to us through the classical repertoire, something she swore she was going to spend the rest of her life doing...

"A brilliant transcriptionist she was as well, having gone into the operas of Gioachino Rossini, prepared to come out with so many of his most beautiful works, insisting that Rossini's genius is largely hidden behind the human voices inside his operas and religious works, set in the future to record many of these transcriptions in something she was going to call "The Rossini Project," where she had said, *"the voice of God prophecies to the end of the world...*

"But sadly, the cares of this selfsame world, the tragedy of human existence, which is Fate, the Sorrow of the Ages was heaped upon this wife and mother, this highly respected and gifted lady cellist, who has taught many of the most successful cellists in the world, and who herself was the recipient of every concert and performance award imaginable. Who was very likely about to set the classical world on fire with her beautiful transcriptions and interpretations of the standard repertoire.

"A testament to the effect she had on the world around her can be seen just by a quick glimpse through this sea of mourners we have here today, among whom are some of the most famous musicians in the world. And in keeping with who she was, a woman of few idle words spoken, who delivered her endtime messages through the soul of her instrument, I think it best for us to take the next two minutes to reflect on the voice of divinity she was able to channel through the cello, as we listen to what will be her voice released to the world posthumously, to deliver her endtime message from the Throne of God."

The minister turns silently from the great cathedral pulpit, stepping into the ghost of a melody the world knows so well, spoken through the venerable Cello Suite No. 1, and the voice of eschatology in the Prelude. The sounds of warning sooth and sadden every awestruck listener in the echo chamber of Holies, as the voice of her cello rings out in perfect sound, and the brilliance of one of the smoothest and most sparkling performances of this piece of music ever recorded. The entire cathedral sits in fearfulness and rapture, held prisoner by a warning recorded for the last generations on the face of the Earth, and the spirit poured out upon this flesh, from the Throne of Almighty God.

"*She looks so much like your daughter,*" are the cobra-esque words formed in the air in serpentine, as we mill toward the back of the Great Cathedral. I watch my mother adjust her false face for the task at hand, until it is unmistakably her own, and indistinguishable from the truth. For these poor, ignorant souls, the nosy busybodies who crashed this prestige funeral, always so brilliant in their ability to catch everything of interest anywhere nearby—for these poor souls, I am only my Mother's niece, visiting them for the summer.

"You are your cousin's *twin,*" the rich lady with the deep country accent says, unable to stop staring at me, oddly enough being a woman I remember seeing which, for me, was probably less than a month ago, when her countenance was minus 20 years in perpetuity. The woman did not age anywhere *near* as well as my mother did, her face looking every bit the time passed and then some, as if having carried the burden of her phony life of heavy, perpetual smiles and forced good will had worn her down, exhaustion hidden under the layer of makeup caked on. Though the woman was younger than my mother then, she looks older than my mother now, and coffee-fast thin under her gray mourner's coat and bottle blonded hair. Social worker extraordinaire, Ms. Christine Hopkins, hardly knocking on the door of fifty but looking like she just might have started up the walkway to sixty. A sixty year old woman trying to look under fifty is the impression she delivers, which truly cannot be her fault, as all are not blessed with the beauty pageant bone structure of my actress faced mother.

And I am forced to glimpse into my mother's heart at this moment, where I can see the Amazonian libido in domination, standing behind this shorter, softer, less attractive woman of flopping breasts hidden, bending her over in a bedroom of great secret from behind. Bending her over until the woman must panic and begin to cry out, as only a frightened grown woman can, causing my mother to tremble instantly from her waist down. This soft bodied, flop breasted, pear shaped woman of smiles and doormat sensibilities, so deeply acquainted with what churns beneath cultured civility.

As we near the huge front doors of the cathedral, doors already opened to this 39th straight day of light and heavy east coast rainfall, the Evanopoulos daughter, Adina, steps boldly up beside my sister and takes hold of her arm, teeth blared like a crocodile in a good mood, thanking us for coming, escorting Angela off to the side like the unfortunate victim of a successful kidnapping. Mother is unable to look away from the scene, watching closely until she sees Adelia's daughter step closer to Angela. And when my sister turns to walk away, her face washed over in confusion and humility, when she is suddenly jerked around by Adina Evanopoulos grabbing her arm in disguised bitterness and aggression, Mother walks the first of these many involuntary steps of involuntary motion, walking in a bit of a hurry toward her daughter's unknown dilemma.

I wander slowly behind her, my heart aflutter when the grab on my sister's arm becomes a hard grab to her wrist, and a bitter, caustic stare and speaking pattern from the lady cellist's oldest daughter. "Is there a problem?" I hear mother say, her head tilted in bewilderment at this young woman's audacity to put her hands so aggressively on her daughter.

"The cello is rightfully mine," Adina says, loudly enough to be noticed. "And I want it back."

"Angela what is she talking about?"

"She gave me her mother's cello right after she died. Now she wants it back. Even though her mother wanted me to have it."

Without a word, and whether in reference to the cello or not, my heart is aflutter again, as is several lookers-on nearby, as my mother grabs *hard* the beautiful Greek woman's hand, wrenching it away from Angela's wrist in total silence. I can hardly believe that in the midst of all these people, at the funeral of a world renown musician, these two women appear to be at the edge of a *physical* confrontation.

But there is something in my mother's look, a look that bears a warrior's stare, the possession of a genuine temper unleashed that backs the hot blooded young Greek woman down in the church, enough for her to remember not to so soon and so publically disrespect her mother's memory. At the edge of a line uncrossed, in the wake of a lit fuse cut away, Adina Evanopoulos is escorted by her younger sister, saying once more "it belongs to *me*," patting herself on the chest in aggressive possession, in angry revocation of her mother's dying wish.

"*Why* didn't you tell me anything about this…*cello?*"

The hesitation in the air around us is wrought with tension, as Angela navigates slowly in the line of mourners on the way to the burial site.

"I asked you a question."

"I… I just didn't… I was waiting until you came inside and saw it yourself. Then I was going tell you where it came from."

From behind them, from my view in the back seat, the dynamic is fascinating to behold, as a 32 year old, independent woman stumbles and fumbles through a lie, in fear of her mother, this beautiful woman in her early 50's staring at her daughter with hardly a breath, and without batting an eye. Suddenly, the older woman reaches out to the younger, causing her to flinch as if she's been touched by a hot needle, though the older woman has simply wiped the strands of silken black hair from her daughter's face. From her daughter's eyes.

The rest of our journey is wrought with tension. The kind that is born from fear. This is Angela's fear that I so easily perceive, a fear born in the fires of post trauma. Memories of a twisted ear, pulled strands of silken hair, the flesh grabbed and twisted at her sides. As mother's hands slide down her hair, over the back of her neck and her shoulders, the caress has nothing of the calming effect it should, but rather causes Angela's nerves to fill her insides with cold and shivering.

The spirit of this burial bears little in common with that of Tamela Wade, as the lofty, high minded feel has spilled out from the Great Northern Virginia Cathedral to this grand cemetery. We park our SUV somewhere in the rain, to disembark our rolling chariot in the storm, drifting in the sea of at least a hundred mourners left over from the funeral, no doubt because among them is the world famous cellist, determined to pay his respects to the very end. The grasses of this cemetery are a little greener, the gravestones a little grander, the forest and prairie field of more spectacular grandeur to behold. We are all gathered underneath the large tent, sheltered from this thirty ninth rainfall, gathered noisily on the tent roof above us, falling down in a wall of water built by nature all around us.

We stand on either side of our mother, several rows behind the family mourners up front nearby the closed coffin, where we can see the two Evanopoulos daughters taking their place in the annals of music history. Standing so importantly nearby the world renowned cellist, minds ablaze with every other thought except whatever love there may have been between them and the mother they must soon leave behind.

As we hear The Beatitudes hearken from the Sermon On the Mount, I can see the bitter contemplation still on the face of the oldest daughter up front, and her growing anger at her mother for leaving her most prized possession to another. *She didn't even leave it to Athena,* are the words that flow from her mind into the rain—*Athena plays the damned cello, for God's sake.* And in the wake of these words are the images that burden the Theater of her Mind, when she confronted her mother seven years ago, about *"that Asian bitch,"* her prized student that she was *"spending way too much time with."* Memory of her mother's growing coldness, eventually hearing her mother call her a *"disrespectful ass,"* which lit the fires of this supposed disrespect to the fullest, making her say to her mother: *"Well, you know what then, Mom? Fuck you!"*

Adina remembers the flurry of blows received from her Amazonian mother, where there was no one there to break the two of them up from this fight, until Adelia was on top of her oldest daughter on the floor, holding her down on her back—holding her there until she had begun to panic from shortness of breath. But this, having brought no quick mercy, being held there by her bigger, stronger mother until satisfactory fear and contrition had been wrought. The memory of this private humiliation burns the Evanopoulos mind, as she stares blankly at her mother's casket, remembering the death of civility between them, wondering where it is that her beloved mother could have gone.

Adina braves the gusts of memory, of when she began to suspect that her mother was having a love affair with her female Asian student. Wishing so desperately to catch them in the act, to appease the spirit of suspicion, to confirm what it was that she already knew.

The spirit of the cello dances above her mother's grave, and into her fervent memory, as the trauma of that day threatens to reach out to her from the gray, from beyond the mists of pouring rain. Adina cannot be free of the otherworldly sounds coming from her mother's room that day, the sounds of a woman's suffering, whose voice is held captive in the throes of weeping, at the edge of a wailing cry that threatens devastation. Adina cannot be free of her mother's deep, mournful wailing, sounding as though she were wounded at a place too deep to be rescued, in a manner too profound to be saved. Adina cannot forget the sounds that beckon, the sounds of a woman being tormented to pleasures beyond endurance, drawing her up the stairs in quick, quiet tiptoeing steps, as if it would even be possible for her to be heard over the racket. Adina is still a prisoner of her mother's voice, a lone voice crying in the wilderness, in the barren landscape of her soul's recollection, on the eve of the Second Coming.

Adina is held prisoner by the sounds that beckon, that call her up the stairs of her mother's palatial, early afternoon home that was supposed to be devoid of eyes that spy. Adina takes every new step in the fear of the ages, not knowing what to expect, or what it is she can possibly do about it. She takes every new step in reticence, in her soul's preparation for this attack, hearing the sound of her mother's moan so blessedly, so unblessedly louder, calling from a bedroom door left so blessedly, so unblessedly ajar. Adina takes these last few steps in reserve, to serve the demon Curiosity, and the killing that must take place from it when it is satisfied. She takes the last few steps in quiet revelation, hearing the sound of flesh slapping now underneath her mother's wailing, a voice so utterly committed to its purpose, to relieve the suffering of its victim, and to maintain their balance of wit and sanity.

And Adina must now take her place among the unfortunate, of those who have seen sights that they cannot un-see, sights of the profoundly forbidden, as she is witness to the private act of a woman's greatest need met, the privacy of her satisfaction, as she stands *naked* in the middle of the floor, pressed tightly back against a beautiful young Asian woman, who is repeatedly slamming her hands upon two of the largest breasts in God's Creation, slapping and squeezing them both in rhythm from behind, as Adina's mother leans back against the Asian woman, the mother with her eyes closed and her mouth open, being carried to places that few have ever known, enduring pleasures in her body ignited by the forbidden.

Adina cannot escape the sounds of her mother's weeping, the melody of her voice, carried by the rhythm of her breast flesh being slapped so rhythmically and so repeatedly, the sight of her mother's extreme and impossible shapeliness exposed in the daylight hour—the sight and sound of her heavy, gigantic breasts being slapped and squeezed in this rough rhythm, the hybrid of pain and pleasure in her voice, where the pain is slowly being conquered by heights of pleasure unknown.

Oh, Adina, what unique and wonderful sighting is this, this UFO of human expression you see! What in God's name are they doing, my dearest Adina, that sends your mother to the heights of such pleasure and pain! But the fear in your body is too profound, is it not? And you cannot maintain your forbidden place under the sun, in the shadows of daytime dark, near the doorway of your mother's upper room.

You turn and try to desperately escape the approaching Tsunami, the rising tidal wave of the wailing, weeping voice that threatens, the explosion of sound and energy that looms. You run, Dear Adina, as the sound of her Witch's Crown fills the house in mourning, in the sorrow of a weeping devastation, that sings her body electric indeed, and devastates every watchful, awestruck spirit to ruin. You drown in the sorrow of your mother's crashing wave, as you run from the house like the woman running from Hitchcock's farmhouse of terror in *The Birds,* making it out of the house and to your car before you swoon and faint from the loss of breath...

Speeding away in your car and back to parts unknown, prepared to lie to your mother about being unable to visit, unable to drive fast enough to escape the memory of what you just saw, and the resounding echo of what you heard. Unable to escape the requisite pulling over of your car, stepping out of it so that you can breathe, praying to God that your nausea will not rise to completion.

Now, you must brave this memory, my dearest Adina, and burn it into yourself, so that it may become a part of thee. The more you fight its power, the more you will suffer from here to eternity.

A flash of lighting. A blast of sound. A single flinch pricks collectively this crowd of mourners, leaving nerves unraveled, in the aftermath of rolling thunder.

Highways of Lost Hopes and Dreams

$\mathcal{W}$e traverse these rainy miles through the Virginia countryside, on the eve of the 40th wind and rain. The world seems poised on the edge of revelation, as this self same record is being approached in many places around the country, with pockets of local flooding scattered throughout these eastern states and beyond. As we get closer to our country estate, somewhere in the farmlands east of Woodland, I am burdened with the fear of a drowning flood, imagining so easily the possibility of a Worldwide Deluge, and the drowning of every soul in waters risen up to the highest mountain. It seems that God's fury is something vented and displayed in brief flashes, although severely restrained, as much by his promise as his mercy. In the continuous blasts of endtime thunder we hear, in the endless sea of pouring rain, I can feel the love of God beginning to fade, flowing into the other side of his nature, which is the beginning of judgment over mankind. The widespread appearance and intensity of these storms cannot be ignored, storms of tropical force and protracted duration, leaving great stretches of countryside flooded and damaged, to where many roads are becoming impassable; either by barriers of fallen trees, or old and new rivers risen up from one side to the other. And along with the rumbling from the clouds has come a new and more powerful, more tragic rumbling from the ground, with several small fault lines crossing major highways without remorse, sending no one to their graves as of yet, but sparking a message of fear and uncertainty just the same.

The long, asphalt driveway of our property pulls us casually along, rescuing us from the dreary highways of lost hopes and dreams, drawing us into a place of refuge and comfort in the storm. Three of us hurry away from the SUV, one in restrained bitterness, the other two in repressed confusion and fear.

The two of us walk into Angela's house behind our mother, both of us suddenly ill at ease, being that this is the first time she has set foot in this house since the last time she was here over a month ago. Mother slides out of her grand, full length black coat, not even bothering to look as she holds out for one of us to take it and hang it up. Her eyes are drawn to the two cellos on the other side of the big living room, not really caring at all which one of them is the one the Evanopolous ravens were all so noisy about.

"Which one is hers?" she asks.

Falsely.

"You're kidding, right?" Angela answers, a voice replete with repressed reserve and resentment. "The one on the left. Obviously. The one that looks like a London Stradivarius."

"A London *what?*"

"That was played at the Paris Opera in 1868. At the 500th performance of *William Tell.*"

I watch my tall, shapely mother wander over, all shades of gray from her blouse to her shirt, from her belt, buckle, and down to her boots. So deliciously unafraid to monochrome, be it black, navy, wine, forest green, or the various shackles of melancholy gray. The skirt is form fitting all the way down to the dark gray boots, displaying the silhouette of the broad hipped side of feminine power over fifty. Although my sister's haunches, those of the Wade woman we buried, and even my own are noticeably bubbled and spread, the character and form of my mothers' backside is an unusually widened tribute to the hourglass form, so that there are never a pair of hips around her to rival hers in sheer girth and glory. Of any woman that we have ever seen, or that most will ever see, Ja'net Littledove's backside is nearly unrivaled in its dynamic, even by the extraordinary form of the dearly departed Greek cellist, whose waist thickness was just a few too many more inches toward the athletic side, and not as deeply cinched as this woman here that we know. Our Lady of the Hips, she is, in response to her daughter's anointing as a breast queen.

Our Lady strolls, stylish and gray, over to the two beautiful cellos that decorate the living room as a pair, playing whatever unheard duets that are meant for their ghostly ears only.

The two cellos are the difference between talent and inspiration. Where one bears the look of the finer instrument, with a shinier, high gloss dark wood finish, accented by a deep black fingerboard where the strings are strung, with two uniquely elegant, angel figurines carved upon the wood on either side.

"Between now and Friday morning," she says, touching the top of the left cello, the exquisitely crafted, antique object of the Evanopoulos affection, "I want you to go to that school, and give them your notice."

Angela closes the coat closet without looking up, as if she were hearing words formed in real space that she had already perceived somewhere in her spirit. Her expression bears the strength of one who has been hit enough times already, so that the first blow carries little weight of pain or fear.

"Notice for what?"

"What do you usually give an employer a notice for?" she says. Playing the same, no look, no eye contact game.

"How am I going to get tenure Mom, if I take time off?"

"Back talk," Mother says. Still caressing a gentle gaze over the lovely instrument. "That's all I ever seem to get from you these days. Time was, I would have heard a different answer."

Mother finally looks up from the cello. Walking slowly, in the power of her easy command, over to where her two daughters stand in waiting. When she looks away from Angela, staring me directly in the eye, I feel the same level of terror that someone at the top of a giant roller coaster feels.

"Go up to Angela's closet, Caley. Bring the black suitcase sitting to the right."

"Yes Ma'am."

I turn and move as quickly as I can up the stairs without breaking into a full run, as though I may be on the edge of an invisible lash or two.

"You have a higher calling, Angela. Something greater than being a lowly science professor at some oversize state college. Things are different now. Your father and I are worth more money than what you could be worth in ten lifetimes on your own. And whether you want it or not, your calling is to be a part of that. To become fully engrossed, if you will. Fully a part of our family's 'fortune.' Which means that you will do what I say. When I say it. And how I say it. Do you understand?"

As I return down the stairs with the heavy, black suitcase, Angela endeavors to answer Mother, only managing to open and close her mouth quietly. It is only my fumbling presence down the stairs that keeps Ja'net Littledove from stepping forward in this, to remind her lovely Angela Tao Ling that her adopted name is Angela Littledove.

Mother takes the suitcase from me and hauls it over to the sofa, unzipping it, opening it as casually as if it were on a hotel bed on one of her many trips, shocking my already devastated little soul to greater ruin, when I see the length of white rope, a small black whip, black paddle and cane, and the glinting blade of a very long, sharp knife.

As it is written, the types of fear are many, and uniquely distinguished. Among these is the Fear of Pain, which has come to life in the minds of both my sister and me, coursing through every part of us through our blood. Mother leans over the special suitcase, her body displayed with such strength and beauty in gray. She places the length of thin, white ropes on the sofa, and picks up the long, sharp knife. In a fearfulness rivaling what I knew that night, when I was lost on the road to Woodland, I watch the beautiful woman cut a short length of rope with skill and knowledge, walking over to my sister as casually as can be, the expression on her face depressed to such a somber tone as is possible on the up side of a frown.

As Angela stands with her lovely mouth partially open, her eyes glassy in shock and disbelief, mother binds her wrists behind her back tightly, in knotted fashion designed for permanent immobility. Mother then cuts and retrieves another piece of the long, thin white rope, tying it tightly around the top of Angela's arms, binding them tightly behind her back. My sister stands as tall and strong as she can, but thoroughly humiliated, unable to look up from her mother's boots as she cuts and retrieves a third piece of rope, going back to her daughter and tying it around her thighs, just above the knee.

"For the arms, maybe," Mother says, studying the rope across the front of her daughter's black dress. "But for the legs…"

She goes back to her suitcase kit, and retrieves a black leather strap, securing it to her daughter's legs in tighter fashion, then cutting the ill advised leg rope away. She kneels down to the floor, and wraps the rope instead around her daughter's legs above the ankles, tying it tight and secure.

"Caley," she says. Gently. "Bare your sister's breasts."

"Mother, please," are the words that flow from Angela's mouth, as I go over to her and unbutton her black blouse, still hardly prepared for the sheer size of the black bra underneath. I lower the straps from her shoulders, drawing strength from her eyes in doing so, reaching inside the bra and, one at a time, slide the gargantuan bosoms out into open space. The massive contrast, the rounded, mountainous breasts exposed, the white skin framed by the black cloth is breathtaking, a monument to the rare beauty of extreme breast growth on a woman, which, although I have already seen, never seemed so exposed and gigantic as they do at this moment.

"And now yours," Mother says. I obey as quickly as I can, pulling my black turtleneck shirt upward, then quickly raising up my bra to let my pink nipples shine. I stand with my shirt up and my eyes lowered, my hands clasped in front, waiting for Mother to perhaps walk up behind me. But I instead hear Angela's pleading voice again, seeing a renewed desperation on her face, which makes me turn and look to see what horror she faces. I see Mother gathered at the Cello of Dreams, the heirloom passed from music legend, raising up one string with one hand, using her long, sharp knife blade to bow it with the other. The string pops and dies in an unknown key of ugliness, which draws a yip from my sister, and a swearing to obedience, and loyalty beyond any given before. But the second, third and fourth strings all die this same death in some tragic minor key, each one building its negative power upon the other in Angela's soul, until her beautiful face is twisted in an ugly cry, which is the beauty of her unfathomable suffering.

I turn away from the sight of the Amazonian female in melancholic gray, walking toward us with her knife firmly in hand, having no idea of what to prepare myself for. Mother steps behind her crying, once sophisticated daughter, who thought she had understood what this woman was all about, and where it is along the timeline she had hearkened from. In terror, I watch her stand behind Angela with this knife, placing it fully to her throat at if to run it across, but stopping at the moment of truth.

"Suck your sister's breasts."

Without hesitation, I reach down and take light hold of one of Angela's monstrous mounds, placing my lips gently, in a light, kissing suck, as phony as I can possibly make it, as if I am posing for the spirits that stand and watch us nearby. After at least half a minute of this,

Mother places her knife on the arm of the nearest comfort cushioned chair, then gets close behind me.

Of what level of burning pain I feel next, I cannot tell. I only know that the sting of a thousand wasps now pierces my breasts from without, as Mother twists a shriek from my body unbeknownst, of a loudness and pitch I never before believed was possible. A second twisting brings a second scream, along with tears that flow freely, and an admonishment from her to:

"Nurse your sister's breasts like you mean it. Or I swear to God I will make you wish you were *dead.*"

And this, I hear in her deep, breathy voice in my ear, a voice filled with unearthly craving at its peak, a starving hunger awakened and unsatisfied, that arises resentment to contempt, and contempt into pure hatred. She releases both my nipples in the hard, biting pull of legend, causing me to wince and sob at what possibilities there be, in the revelation of just what pain really is.

"Now you know where the pleasure stops," she says. "And where the pain starts."

She retrieves her knife again, returning to her place behind her crying, Asian eyed daughter.

"Now," she says. "Suck your sister's breasts."

And this, I do. Understanding now that the feel of Angela's nipples in my mouth is the catalyst for relief, the satisfaction of a phantom thirst, the redemption of lost hope for this life, the salvation of our souls in this gloomy twilight.

"You'll do this to her every day," she tells me, "until the day you can taste the milk."

This, the call of the nursemaid, I hear. As Mother takes the knife, and begins to cut away my stunned sister's restraints, I know that she has been called and chosen to become a wet nurse to my mother's perversion. Something far greater than what she had considered in all these years of my sister's suffering. It is her inspiration, her calling realized, to begin me on this selfsame path, that she may have two outlets for her hunger and thirst to alleve.

"Cover her," she says. I gladly obey, covering myself first, and then helping her slide back into her big bra, so that she can begin to button her blouse again. I notice that Angela's fingers are trembling just a bit, and the look on her face is the anguish of post trauma.

"You'll call me when you've quit that job," she says. "And I'll be by every few days, to check to see if your milk has come in. Oh, and if you have that bitch's cello restrung, or whatever they call it, before I give you permission, I'll chop it into little pieces and burn it."

And then, Mother suddenly walks over to the grieving Angela, and whispers deeply, profoundly in her ear, something that sends her sorrow to another place of bereaving, to a place of such deep agony within her spirit that it causes her to wince in physical pain.

I am then shocked into wide eyed wonder, when Angela picks up the knife from the nearby chair when my mother's back is turned, and we are all shocked into three shrieks of their own making, as Angela jabs the blade deep into Mother's lower back, causing her eyes to go wide with terror, as she reaches around to try and pull it out, managing only to turn around and fall to her knees, grabbing Angela on the way to the floor, her voice moaning a sickening groan, as she tries to crawl to the front door, the blade stuck so firmly in her lower back, and the bottom of her gray blouse blackened with a growing spot of blood.

The Tilling of the Soil

In the shadows of disbelief. In the glaring light of truth. In our soul's pain of shock and terror. We stand awestruck at the foot of the stairs, at the base of this mountain peak of tragedy. The statuesque and beautiful woman, the source of what life we had, lies at the door outward from this life, her life's blood slowly oozing away.

The two of us stand still, breathless in waiting, to see the beautiful blonde woman in gray stir a leg, twitch a finger, moan an inner cry for help. But instead, we are met with a flash of lightning and blast of thunder from the clouds, to coincide with the appearance of a growing pool of blood, to the right side of the body where she lays. Instinctively, the two of us know that there is no 911 to call, and no other human being on earth to trust, unless we wanted to give away our freedom to the demons that have come to collect it.

No.

We are held captured in the spots where we stand. Barely able to move, barely able to breathe, barely able to think beyond the barrier of this moment, and its implications into our immediate future.

I am finally able to move my head, enough to turn and look desperately at my sister, who seems as if the spirits are gathering her up for an adjustment, to feed her strength to deal with this tragedy, the otherworldly trauma of an altered destiny.

"What did she say?" I ask, which prompts only a shaking of her head, as if I have asked a question that the heavens have forbidden. "Angela, please. Mom is dead. What did she say to you?"

She turns her gaze from our mother in such epic, slow determination, a head turn so deliberate as to have force and power. I think it is the burden of fear and confusion on my face that slams so hard at the gate of her resolve, until I can sense that somewhere inside, she is grieving to tell me why.

"I need to hear it, Angela," I say, blinking away the haze of tears, not caring that they cause the severest tickle on my face. "I need to know."

Angela turns her gaze away, not quite as slowly as before, back to the woman with the kife so deeply in her lower back, laying beside the now massive pool of blood.

"She whispered to me," Angela says, "she whispered *'Caley is an abomination. She cannot be allowed to live. After I drink your milk, she dies.'*"

In the shadows of disbelief. In the glaring light of truth. I stand in the devastation of awe again, my hand over my mouth. Newly acquainted with the third part of the Truth.

Which is cataclysm.

*T*he third victim of this storm of eschatology lies wrapped in the white sheet on the wet, woodsy ground, as Angela and me remove the last shovelfuls of Earth from her grave, giving full credence to the phrase *six feet under.* We make easy work of the soft, Virginia soil, grateful for the thick canopy of trees above us, that partially protect us as we dig into the damp earth in the evening.

When the last muddy shovelfuls of clay have come and gone, Angela tosses the *brand new shovel* out of the grave. I slide the body to the edge of the open grave where she does what she can to lower our mother's body down inside. *To keep animals from digging her up*, she had said, as we had spent the long hours chopping and digging, to where the term "shallow" could not be applied here. Angela and me lower the stiff, heavy body down into the open grave, where the white sheet is now filthy in the corruption of its calling.

I take hold of my sister's hand, pulling her up and out of the grave for the last time. Without a word spoken, we both set to work with our *brand new shovels,* until the echoes of white are completely covered, and every shovelful of dark'ned earth raises the ground upward, until this hole in nature's space is filled in, and the body in the soil is buried six feet away. We finish our work tirelessly, smoothing out the earth as much as we can in the dark, appreciating the many strange, bright rivers of lightning that have begun to crawl under the bottom of the early nighttime clouds. What work there is left at our mother's grave must be finished tomorrow, as we answer the calling voice in the nighttime storm, to leave the soil of our evil deed behind for the night.

The tools of our conquest rest nearby the freshly dug grave, as we take hands in the drowning mist of rain, walking fearlessly together in the drunkenness of exhaustion, in the stormy haze of mysteries unrevealed. We take each breath on the other side of this barrier crossed, feeling the rain on our faces as a shower of renewal in the night. As the rivers of lightning crawl underneath the clouds, the wind touches us as a breath of renewal, as the clouds flash in gentle brightness all over the sky without ceasing, to illuminate the mercy of this brief, rainy reprieve in the storm.

Like two phantoms, like two souls of the undead, we make our way from the edge of the darkened woods, crossing the great lawn toward the house, feeling the relief of privilege when we finally reach the back patio door, sliding it open and walking so casually inside, as though we were engaged in nothing beyond the tilling of the soil, and the burial of sapling roots in a rose garden.

The disappearance of our mother prompts an investigation of sorts, a formality of milling around by authorities—questions asked gone unanswered, the natural assumption of foul play, and the perpetual wondering of where her body may be, after her SUV was found in the rushing waters of a woodsy ravine. My poor father has accepted this next comeuppance overdue in stride, as all successful people seem to be able to do, when money talks and bullshit walks. Money has the calming effect of anesthesia. It is the greatest earthly cure for what ails us after love has failed, and when friends and family have come and gone. Ray Littledove can hardly wait for the time to pass, when his wife's stinking corpse will emerge somewhere in the Virginia woods underneath these raging floodwaters, so he can set about the task of securing another pair of tits to suck and fuck.

How long would it be for a rich lawyer to be widowed, before the alley cats come crawling? Cats of every size, shape and color, hoping to help the rich lawyer forget all his troubles, and the wife who just might be dead and gone. Angela and I languish in the aftermath of this storm, unburdened by guilt as much as grief and confusion over what has transpired. Somewhere in our hearts and minds, the act occurred outside of ourselves, as if an unseen force was drawn in because of her past sins, and saw to it that she was judged and condemned. The pain of remorse is glaringly absent, replaced by the pain of fear and dread, of nosy, gifted detectives and cadaver dogs and luminol, and the two of us in two separate prisons somewhere in the world. But even while these fears come and go, even while they manifest themselves day and night, I can already sense a time of renewal for us, where the pain of her memory will be the only burden from her left to endure.

We walk arm in arm with her, the two of us, up and down the timeline from where she was born and raised in depravity, to where she sent this spirit so completely down onto the mind, body and spirit of my sister, to my brief and deadly introduction to the power of what she hath done. I am well aware of the irony of her life and death, that while she heaped pain upon torture onto her daughter over the years, she was in fact heaping coals of fire onto her own head. She may just as well have died by her own hand, as by the hands of her beautiful and sophisticated daughter, who could not have imagined having done such a careless and brutal thing, were it not driven into her slowly, bit by bit over the years, where it finally blossomed into a rage of insanity.

As we run our little life errands in the gray, securing Daddy's Money, restoring the heirloom cello string, planting a new tree in the woods, in the soil of our discontent, the truth is we are still burdened by the power of her memory, and the force of her depravity passed on 'til perpetuity.

How much is it to our mother that we owe, when Angela is bent over the kitchen counter fully nude, gigantic breasts mashed onto the counter top, while I stand behind her in strapped on, 16 year old girl determination? How much do we owe this to our mother, that a 32 year old woman suffers this craving, to be manhandled by her sixteen year old sister to completion? Every inch times eight pushed deep into her womb from behind, myself stripped as naked as she? Do the sounds that she makes hearken from her days and years, when she herself was strapped on as I am, with our mother bent over the kitchen table in like manner, yelling a war cry into the walls of secret?

Does Angela remember this from her sixteen year old self, soon after our mother had discovered the power of her daughter's kiss? By what energy do I work myself into this angry rhythm, so determined to see her crumble, to see and hear her annihilation, from the explosion of energy within? Standing up behind her in the kitchen, by what energy do I pound into her with the force and power of a moving train? By what spirit do I grab onto, holding on tight to both of my sister's gargantuan breasts as she screams?

The blood of Christ reigns supreme over lost humanity. This, in the midst of our depravity in the foothills of the Blue Ridge Mountains, on both sides of every evening day. The two of us move forward in our natural progression, from our earlier time at the kitchen, to the soft intimacy of her bedroom, overlooking the back lawn of our best laid plans gone awry. Again, as I massage the two great melons from behind, it begs to wonder, as to the true source of her breast centered secret life, the beginning and the end of what we do, which has grown in focus and intensity since the burial of the three Mothers, in this storm off Melancholy Bay.

From what part of the timeline doth her soul share in proximity, as I stand behind her, burying both hands into the great globes of flesh, feeling her body react as if being given a medicine for what ails it? This natural breast sensitivity is as a bolt of lightning, hearkening from the far east, from the natural blood by which she was born.

Lai Ling Tao, the country poverty beauty, the source of these two great breasts I hold in my hand, the source of this magic breast sensitivity, this unique link from the nipple to the groin. This, a unique and powerful breast touch, which has plagued Angela for most of her life, from early adolescence, when they were already bigger than most grown women when she was thirteen. A condition awakened further in part by my mother, but then held back and suppressed by the dispensation of pain rather than pleasure. Then, brought to maturity by the breast goddess Adelia, the lady cellist who now haunts the world in spirit. But Adelia's breast centeredness was so rushed and so exclusively focused on her own mountains, due to their brief time and limited space together. What powerful feeling it is that Angela was capable of was only touched upon by her two tormentors, neither of who fully understood the depth of her feeling, squeezing and pulling and pinching and sucking too hard or too soft, and never long enough or in the right frame of mind for herself— always so focused on giving the mothers their pleasure, and never able to concentrate on receiving hers. Never able to dominate any session that focused on how she felt, or what she needed to feel completely fulfilled. The legion of little twitches and microspasms she had were brief and orgasmic, to be sure, but as the sensitivity in her breasts begins to awaken, she realizes that she may have never felt the fullest explosion of her body's potential, as achieved through the stimulation of her breasts alone.

As I massage her from behind, amazed at the length of time she asks, I can feel her mind's deep and growing concentration, and her soul's exploration of what full pleasures there are to be wrought. She refuses to speak, refusing to tell me how right or wrong my clumsy, heavy squeezing and pinching are, but she is satisfied to rest on the journey of exploration, to put herself in my hands, so to speak, to put herself in her sister's hands, to learn of what road there is to take, and how far along that road she must travel.

Is it the Licking Road? The flicking of the tongue at her nipples? The heavy, ice cream lick, or the light, lollipop lick? Is the dry licking, the abrasion of the tongue against them, to watch their slight erectness grow to monumental proportions? Or is the Wet Lick? The licking in the throes of spittle, feeling the tongue in sliding across her nipple? Where else upon her breasts is the greatest sensitivity beyond the nipple? Underneath? Around the sides? At the top, or in between? How far up and down the cleavage must my tongue travel, to cause the rise and fall of her desire?

In the passing of Indian Summer, at the age of 33, Angela Tao begins to play new melodies upon the 36J chord, upon these instruments designed for such power of exploration, born from a woman cursed to return to full poverty in China when Angela was a baby, a woman who explored her breast gift with sisters Angela never knew from when they were 10 years old, games that were mature by the time her four blood sisters were 13 on the farm, when Lai Ling Tao exposed her Special K's to the secret walls of their little farmhouse, letting them swing free above her waist and poverty skirt still on, knowing full well that soon, as she holds her nipple to her 13 year old daughter's nipple, rubbing it like a cavewoman trying to start a fire, that the fire will soon be lit in her body, and the sound she'll make will be tantamount to a weeping, when her grieving body starts to tremble.

The Two Cellos

"*The end of the world may be more of a reality than a philosophy. Whether or not you believe in God or the Bible is largely irrelevant. Especially when we consider the very real possibility that these near misses that keep happening, are indicators that the big one is lurking out there somewhere, just waiting to strike. If Jupiter and Shoemaker-Levy can be taken into account, eventually we'll have to accept the possibility, the reality even, that its more than likely that the same thing could happen to us…*"

And what of the Milking Road, Professor Tao? This, the Nursing Road, the Sucking Road taken. Perhaps, this is your highway to heaven. Your road to your body's greatest pleasure, and intimate treasures unknown. It seems that the two of us travel this road the most. It being the beginning, middle and end of most of what we do in secret. But I have noticed in Angela a deeper concentration, a more profound reaction to the sucking upon her nipples, requiring that I stay on them so much longer than before, where a half hour's time is no stranger to our travels down this path. Of this, we have already seen her embrace, being able to bring herself to completion from this act alone. And it seems that this part of Mother's dark prophecy is about to be carried out, as she tells me to "nurse them like you're trying to drink the milk," betraying the secret desperation she feels to have it happen. To have her already gargantuan breasts swollen bigger with milk, so that she can explore the depth of her heart's deviance, to study the way and manner that it comes forth, whether it runs or drips on its own, learning how to spray it freely into my face and open mouth, to nurse me until I am full, to sit with the two of us in bare nakedness so it can be done, or to have us be fully clothed by contrast, to study the heights and depths of feeling from each path chosen. Along this road, along the Nursing Road, we walk tonight, having spent many days and nights already engaged in the deep nursing of her tits, until both of us wonder if it can indeed truly happen without pregnancy. But truthfully, I myself have become so accustomed to it that I am addicted, so often having to grind my lower body in repose, against her while her nipple is pulled so deeply into my mouth.

And this, I do at this moment in our time, laid underneath her in grinding motion, with her great, hanging breasts pulled down in the vacuum sucking, until I suddenly am aware of a new sensation at the back of my throat, where it is not merely the watering of my mouth and a benign phantom swallow, but the instinct of a big *gulp* which surprises the both of us at once, causing me to release the nipple and look up at it, watching the milk drip steadily from her nipple with the same awe as if I were staring at the night sky, and the approach of an end of the world comet from the Great Beyond.

The taste of Angela's milk is a sweet addiction. The feel of it on my face, or anywhere on my skin, even as it is sprayed or dripped down to my own breasts in silken white. The feel of it on my hands when we take the Squeezing Road, the highway of heft, the mountain road of massage, when I am behind her either in standing or on our knees, squeezing them in full as though the milk will not appear, but being so pleasantly surprised every time when it begins to run down my hands like water from a wet sponge. And it seems that her great globes are heavier than ever, raising her breasts up to an incredible double-J cup from the ridiculous J they already were, yes, nursing bras measured out to a 36 *double* J cup, making Angela Tao one of the most conspicuously busty women on the planet, I think, breasts that she must endeavor to keep hidden in her loose blouses and shirts, sacrificing shapeliness in her clothing for the cause of modesty. Content, as she has been since she was sixteen, to appear heavier in her clothes, so that people might mistake her bosoms for extra weight alone, for if she were to wear typical, form fiting clothes in public, she would surely be a conversation piece for the ages, a big-tittied Asian beauty, the object of so much respect or ridicule. On the beach, in a body suit or a bikini, Angela Tao would be the last word on heavy breasted beauty, and the revelation of what lies beneath would surely be a sign of the times. When she had Adelia's cello repaired, I remember thinking of what eternal source of photographic inspiration this Asian woman's cleavage would be, and how quickly her cello CD's would fly off the classical shelves because of the covers alone.

"You're gonna have to learn to play the piano," she says. "So we can play duets 'til the end of time." But Fate is the chooser of what duets there are to be played. Ours is a duet of depravity. Obsessive, breast centered lust that has threatened to spill outside these walls of isolation, when she once asked me to go with her into the stall of a restaurant bathroom, which I very nearly considered just for her, but was held back in fear at the moment of truth. Somehow, I know that the energy of what we do must be confined to the halls of our secret palace, so that none could ever suspect what these two sisters share in private.

At this moment, we share a walk down the Squeezing Road, where she sits comfortably on the edge of the bed, with me on my knees behind her, her little blonde tit-slave, squeezing and spraying the milk from both breasts at the same time, watching it dampen the carpet below. Then Angela stands up and turns to me, and I sit at the edge of the bed, taking the great breasts into my hands, facing them head on, letting the milk spray into my face until it drips from my chin to my own exposed breasts down below. Angela watches me do this in rapt attention, pulled along this Road with every squeeze and pull of her nipple, until I see her face anguish from the sudden rise of energy inside, as her body twitches once in full, from the bolt of lightning that strikes from her nipple to her groin.

56

*T*he summer rains that died on their 40th day have returned to our country landscape, gathered up in the winds of this gray, November chill. There must be an eschatological exception to every rule, as it is written, "there's no thunder in a November Rain," this exception being a November rain decorated by frequent flashes of invisible lightning lighting up the clouds, and the occasional heavy rumble of thunder across the countryside.

"We should start looking for your real mother," I say, as the spirit of complacency begins to creep in, to replace the creeping spirits of remorse and regret that have haunted us for these many weeks since it happened.

"I was actually thinking the same thing," she says, popping a grape tomato in her mouth at the sink, as she prepares the lettuce and tomato part of our impending taco feast. At the sink, Angela's form is female empowerment in her navy stretch capris, and matching midnight blue sports bra beautifully worn, to fully reveal herself as one of the natural wonders of the world. Every little step and turn this Asian beauty makes is truly a sight to behold, one that would have to be seen to be believed.

"I'll call Dad about it tonight," she says. "Maybe he can— "

Suddenly, we hear a loud *thump* from the front room, seeming to accompany the latest rumble of thunder, as if something had slammed hard against the huge bay window. We both glance bewilderedly at one another, with me wondering what bird has flown into the window and broken its fool neck.

We are both stopped in our tracks when we get two thirds of the way to the window, nearby the two cellos sitting idly by, when a flash of this strange, November lightning lights up the glass, to reveal two muddy *handprints* smudged on the glass, the mud smeared downward a great distance toward the bottom.

"No...fucking... way..." she says, shaking her head 'no,' taking me by the hand. "Dear God in Heaven, don't let it—"

A shriek escapes my pathetic, white girl form, in full W.A.S.P sound and regalia, as the loud *thumping* we heard is transformed to the front door, resounding like an explosion of thunderous noise crashing through the house. The otherworldly strength of whatever it is, is bound and determined, and judging by the sound we hear, its entrance by this doorway is inevitable. Every monstrous slamming into the door evokes another shriek from me, until Angela puts her arm around my waist in full strength, touching her hand gently to my mouth, until I am able to stand without making a sound above a whimper.

Angela whispers powerfully into my ear, and I go immediately to the kitchen to gather a tool of hope and conquest, then heading in desperation toward the back patio door. But I am frozen at the back door for just a moment, when the crashing of splintered wood takes shape and form, as a ghostly hand and arm breaks through the thick wood…

I am unable to move, as the remainder of the door is crashed open intact, shattering the place at the frame where it was locked, to reveal the grisly, mud covered truth of this nightmare we are in. As the angry filth, the corrupted rage of decomposed life stumbles with singular purpose into our space, I hear Angela scream in warrior tone my name and the words "Go, now!" Breaking me from this end of the world spell and stupor of fear I am in. I am privileged enough to not be present at this starting gate, this gate that leads through the barrier between hope and the end of this age, which is the coming end of human history.

Angela turns in the shock of revelation, pricked to her heart by a terror unknown, when this creature lumbers with alarming speed towards her, its eyes glowing white with fury and merciless intent, its corrupted mouth open in the agony of death endured. Angela turns and runs in the haze of icy fear, privy to the sound of a husky, moaning wail of reality, approaching her from behind as she runs in full, Amazonian curves toward the back door, shrieking when the cold, muddy fingers touch the back of her neck as she escapes into the rain.

In the midst of the great lawn, in the mist of this cold, twilight rain, Angela feels the strength of a thousand evils grasp her about the throat, clutching her on the arm without mercy, pulling her to the ground in the stench of rotten flesh, and the wet, scratchy grains of freshly dug-through mud and clay.

Somewhere in the rainy evening, under the clouds lit up with the storm's energy, I hear the sound of my name screamed in hopelessness and otherworldly terror, as the Fear of Death and Hell burns bright, and uniquely distinguished. Angela continues to scream as I arrive, grabbing the thing by what is left of its head of muddy, *blonded* hair, pulling its head backward in brief distraction, allowing Angela to crawl away from its attempt to crush her under the weight of its corruption, and begin to choke the life from her.

When Angela is free from the muddy, half rotted creature of the Autumn Woods, I take my place in the course of these events, as per my sister's brave inspiration, splashing a gallon of *gasoline* onto the crawling thing's back, as it grabs my sister again by the ankle, as she bravely kicks and tries to get away. I hear my name screamed into the night again, along with the words *"Do it now!"* yelled in battlefield terror, and I strike the lighting tool aflame, pressing it to the hair doused with fuel, lighting this living death on fire in the rain. The flames burst into life exponentially, causing the thing to scream a ghostly wail, becoming immobile as its entire body bursts into flame from head to toe.

I hurry over to where my sister stands battle worn, battle ready, both of us gazing in awe as a white form of mist tinted blue takes shape in the fire, risen up from the body and through the flames, disappearing into the rain, as we stand immobilized by what we have seen, as the flames burn the remaining flesh of this thing, rising in fire and vapour of smoke into the storm of this coming night.

Pacific Island

Ground

My eyes are the color of the Caribbean Sea. Of this truth, I remember, as I think back upon my own reflection.

The tropical sunlight bathes us in the warmth of renewal, as we disembark our windy chariot, in the Pacific islands so many thousands of miles from the road to Woodland. My sister and me step peacefully from the plane, into the warm breath of this tropical breeze, so glad to be free from the plague, the vague shadow of her memory.

We take the airplane steps down to the paved, Pacific island ground below, happily receiving the lei's from the exotic hostesses, and the angelic kisses upon the cheek. We walk calmly, quietly, in nervous apprehension to the airport lobby, hardly knowing what to expect.

But truth in revelation is devastation to the soul. Inside the airport lobby, Truth stands up from where it sits in waiting, a truth that inhabits the sunny, warm tropical refuge of this space in voluptuous, unsophisticated beauty, as if she were a projection of my sister come to life from 20 years in the future.

Angela briefly forgets that I exist, as she hurries to the beautiful Asian woman, hugging her tight, and letting the tears flow in slow, steady streams.

ABOUT THE AUTHOR

Jonathan Lovejoy is a graduate of the University of North Carolina at Greensboro, with a B.A. in Religious Studies, and a graduate of Liberty University with an M.A. in Theological Studies. He currently lives in Winston Salem, North Carolina.

For more info on the author's life and career, visit jonathanlovejoy.com